THE TROUBLE WITH BEING BORN

THE TROUBLE WITH BEING BORN

JEFFREY DeSHELL

TUSCALOOSA

The University of Alabama Press
Tuscaloosa, Alabama 35487-0380

Copyright 2008 by Jeffrey DeShell
First Edition

Published by FC2, an imprint of the University of Alabama Press, with
support provided by Florida State University and the Publications Unit
of the Department of English at Illinois State University

Address all editorial inquiries to: Fiction Collective Two, Florida State
University, c/o English Department, Tallahassee, FL 32306-1580

⊗

The paper on which this book is printed meets the minimum require-
ments of American National Standard for Information Sciences—Per-
manence of Paper for Printed Library Materials, ANSI Z39.48–1984

Library of Congress Cataloging-in-Publication Data
DeShell, Jeffrey.
    The trouble with being born / by Jeffrey DeShell. — 1st ed.
       p. cm.
    ISBN-13: 978-1-57366-141-6 (pbk. : alk. paper)
    ISBN-10: 1-57366-141-4 (pbk. : alk. paper)
    1. Marriage—Fiction. 2. Domestic fiction. I. Title.
    PS3554.E8358T76 2008
    813'.54—dc22
                                        2007039820

Book Design: Andrew Farnsworth and Tara Reeser
Cover Design: Lou Robinson
Typeface: Garamond
Produced and printed in the United States of America

Peter: An (A)Historical Romance, 2006

S & M, 1997

The Peculiarity of Literature: An Allegorical Approach to Poe's Fiction, 1997

In Heaven Everything Is Fine, 1991

Chick-Lit 2: No Chick Vics, co-editor, 1996

Chick-Lit: Postfeminist Fiction, co-editor, 1995

I am extremely grateful to the following for their affection and intellectual, artistic and emotional support during the composition of this book: Robert Steiner, Lynne Tillman, Marco Breuer, Ted Pelton, Marcia Douglas, Sidney Goldfarb, Dana Hoey, Karen Jacobs, Sarah Gerstenzang, Michael Gerstenzang, R.M. Berry, Katherine Eggert, John-Michael Rivera, Laura Mullen, Mark Winokur, Jane Garrity, Stephanie Sheffield, Laird Hunt, John Stevenson, John Allen, Carole Maso, Ann Lauterbach, Patricia Ackerman, Brenda Mills, Raymond Federman, Jill Heydt-Stevenson, Patrick Greaney, Brian Evenson and Jim Ackerman. I would like to thank my students, from whom I learned a great deal, especially Sanae Yamada, Benjamin Whitmer, Olivia Chadha and Salma Monani. I would also like to thank my father and the memory of my mother. Finally, I would like to thank Elisabeth Sheffield, who gave me the courage to attempt this book in the first place, and whose love and talent sustain an important part of me. And whose writing takes my breath away. This book is dedicated to her.

"We do not rush toward death,
we flee the catastrophe of birth,
survivors struggling to forget it."

E. M. Cioran
De l'inconvénient d'être né

"With His blessings from above
Serve it generously with love
One man, one wife
One love through life
Memories are made of this
Memories are made of this"

"Memories Are Made of This," Dean Martin
Words & Music by Terry Gilkyson,
Richard Dehr & Frank Miller

MOTHER

Sunshine...everyone open your books...I did my best...
hair...my hair...hands on my head washing...don't yell...stop
yelling...who is this Frances is this your son...ditto cabbage
head ditto...mother...we'd better get back...stop it Joe...a
pinwheel in the light...cotton candy...he called me pretty...
handsome...I have to feed the chickens...I don't believe so...
how much do you weigh...three hundred pounds...count-
ing...Fulbright...he chased me on a horse trying to knock
me down...hotdog...sunshine outside...it hurts...where is
my mother...breast...three times seven is twenty one four
times seven is twenty eight...Jay brought over some of Ted's
clothes...maybe you could...leave him alone...I hoped we'd
have a sister but your dad...mistakes...washing dishes I'm
so tired...blond boys next door playing with yellow trucks...
shame on you shame on me...Aunt Helen...don't sit under
the apple tree with anyone else but me...skating...toes cold
I have to go to the bathroom...Chinese chicken salad...don't
like coke...Lucky Strike means fine tobacco...too fat...peas
milk and purple juice...it hurts...stooped shoulders...he was
ashamed...of me...Billy Graham...Steve...alone...don't eat
it if you don't like it...pork chop fried chicken mashed potatoes...outside...sunshine...and...can't...remember...John

11

Elway…south girls won…what to cook tonight…so many flowers red and white carnations yellow daisies blue columbines…he was allergic to dust…always a good boy…red Jell-O…no thank you…no thank you…Doctor Mastro…you should eat something in the morning…how much did you spend…my brother offered me a ride back to the house on the tractor…why did he make Star scream…stop it you two stop fighting or I'm leaving…Dominic and his girls…maybe you could try computers or something…it took me hours to fix dinner and you gobble it up in five minutes…let me stand up…horse pills…make the coffee…her hands on my head a little water running down my neck…white linen…Archie Bunker…does she recognize you…Frances Patterson 11145 Route 6 Barry Illinois…is that you…Wal-Mart Kmart King Soopers Safeway…I love you too Jeff…what is her name…ouch…ouch…playground duty…mimeograph machine I like the smell…a hateful face… she always cleans her plate…you need to write a thank-you note…what have I done…five is aqua blue seven is pearl white three is pale rose…I don't like to drive the blue car…Auntie Virginia was here…I looked up Budapest on the map…why didn't they put his picture with the description…I'll get the wooden spoon…I smell funny…I'm tired of spaghetti every Sunday…our father who art in heaven hallowed be thy name… no I don't want any wine…they have a big motor home and they drive everywhere…I finally bought a new coat it was on sale…I'm tired…oh a run in my stocking…your hair used to be so curly…we'll have to take out a loan for tuition…I don't know Joe I don't know…the new riverwalk down where Ted's shop used to be…this is what a gimlet tastes like…a lump in my breast…can you remember what day it is Frances…Folger's is almost a dollar more…Columbo sure is smart…this sweet corn is tasty…April May June July…Jimmy wants to be a fireman and drive a firetruck...I looked at the teacher's directory and I didn't recognize anyone but Mrs. Anderson...Mrs. Haslett at the Minnequa Bank...your scout trip back east...why did you tear up my flowers you old mean man you mean old cabbage head...you're very welcome Frances...we don't have the money...did you remember your trombone...good night sleep tight until we meet again...I'm hungry I'm always hungry...I can't remember what that thing is called...my underwear is sticky...move down the hall...the woman who smiles has apples on her desk...cereal has gotten so expensive...visit my cousin Harry...my brother's wife had red hair and died soon after...Mrs. Tate across the street...all he talks about is the war...I like the chicken tacos here...I know where you've been you smell...Jeff writes books...blue is hot and red is cold...come here Star come here little doggie...father was exhausted from digging twelve hours a day...the only boy in my elementary education class...Flo and I took the Greyhound all over...the television is broken...my leg hurts...where is her baby she had it yesterday...I like that colored man on *60 Minutes*...Babe would buy all those fireworks it took hours to set them all off...my mother will be angry...a house exactly like our house...I did my best but I made mistakes...I'm right here stop yelling...Pueblo is hot and dry...where is my lipstick...I can't find anything anymore...life is just a bowl of cherries...don't drive so fast...I don't want to...my girdle is tight...who are you...nuttier than a fruitcake...my doll had black hair...fried chicken...I never cared for Johnny Carson... sprained both of my ankles...those kids with their drugs...ask Mrs. Elizando if you can please borrow four eggs...I'll go in early to put up the bulletin board for Thanksgiving...I have to give Jeff his allergy shot...home made vanilla ice cream at the church...Aunt Helen didn't like him at all...move over

MOTHER

13

here move out of the way...what are those flowers called...it
hurts...left breast prosthesis....new carpet and new furniture...hello Frances...color the map so that the states next to
each other are different colors...Jay bought these dresses for
me...brush your teeth...I'm hungry...it hurts...the chickens
scared him and he fell in some pooh...who was that on the
phone...are my parents dead...what is that...please stop...
do I look okay...go back downstairs...amber necklace from
Turkey...my birthday...out of the way...I wish you were
dead cabbage head...we will come rejoicing...took me to the
movies...he was being nasty...stand up straight...say you're
sorry Larry...this restaurant is expensive...I don't understand
computers...Mexicans blacks and women...I don't think he's
well...I thought my husband paid you...how many times are
you going to read that paper...would you like something to eat
I have sausage baloney pepperoni and Zoelsman's bread...

MOTHER

FATHER

"Frankie. Frankie. Go down to Summit and get me three shorties from Giarantano's, wouldja? Here's a buck. Come back and I'll give ya a quarter. You and your brother can go to the movies or something." "Yes sir." "That's a good kid. You dress nice. You hurry, maybe I toss in an extree nickel. For some soda pop. But don't let nothing happen to the shorties."

Jazzy. Me and Babe can go to the pictures after he gets home from violin practice and we eat. I hope Mama's feeling better. She ain't been the same since she had Dorie. Ange can't make the gravy like Mama. I'm hungry, too.

I like going to Giarantano's for the booze. When I walk back with the paper bag, everyone knows where I've been, and everyone knows I can be trusted. Even though I'm just a kid I look like a big shot. There goes Frankie Fruscella, he's going to be something someday. And sometimes old man Giarantano gives me a nickel. It's like I'm already in business. Maybe I'll give some of the money to my sisters. I can give them a dime, and me and Babe can still go to the movies twice if we don't buy nothing.

I'm glad Secondino didn't ask me to go to Diadosa's. It's on Palm Street, up the hill and across the tracks, near where Occhiatto keeps his goats. No one can see me walk back from there, and it's dusty anyway. And those goats stink. I don't like Diadosa: he acts like we owe him money or something. He acts that way to everyone, it ain't just me. He never gives me a penny, and sometimes he tells me to bring back the bottles. Bring back the bottles! For what? I don't work for you. He's cheaper than Giarantano, though, and father likes his Dago Red better.

Hmmm, smells like Mrs. Tojetti's making sausage again. She puts in too much garlic, marone, it burns your mouth. Smells good now though.

"Hello, Mrs. Giarantano. Hello Mrs. Fanella. Mr. Giarantano, he's out in the shed? Thank you. No, Mama's fine. Thank you. I'll tell her you asked." I like Mrs. Giarantano, but Mrs. Fanella, she's a nosy bitch. Always asking me about Mama. I do like Father says, I don't tell nobody nothing. Another thing about Mrs. Giarantano, she keeps everything spotless. Not like Diadosa's, where you get goat shit all over your shoes walking to the front door. "Hello, Mr. Giarantano. It's me, Frankie Fruscella. Frankie Fruscella. Yeah." They open the door, and I smell the tobacco, the whisky and the men. "Hello Mr. Giarantano, Mr. Garzella, Mr. Bruno. Mr. Secondino sent me: he wants three shorties." I open my palm to Giarantano, who quickly takes the bill without touching my hand. He takes three bottles from a box behind this tool rack, puts them in a used paper bag, and hands it to me. Once, when we were alone, I saw him open up a door in the ground, in the cement, reach in, and drag up a couple of boxes. He looked at me, pointed to his right eye, and shook his head. Mr. Giarantano, he don't say much, but I got the message. I don't care what the coppers would do to me, I wouldn't ratfink on nobody. Not even goat-shit Diadosa. I take the bag, look up for a second, and he just looks back at me. He owes Secondino a quarter. "Thank you,"

I say. He nods. I wait, and then he laughs, digs in his pocket and tosses me the two bits.

I'm crossing Evans when I hear someone calling my name. It's my brother, halfway down the block, running toward me, his violin case bouncing against the side of his leg. At first, I think he's just running because he's hungry and wants to get home, but then I see three or four kids behind him, chasing him and throwing rocks. Bojohns.

I'm carrying three shorties for Secondino, plus I'm in my good clothes and shoes, but what can I do, it's my brother, so I start running down the block toward him. I'm hoping they're little kids, my brother's age, and maybe I can scare them or something. As we get closer, I can see his face and he's pretty scared. "Hey you punks," I yell, "leave him alone." He runs up to me and stops, turns around. The bojohns stop about ten feet away, looking at me. They're younger than me, but big, like bojohns are. Three of them. I wish I had a baseball bat or something. "Zat your brother?" "Yeah, what's it to you? Why don't you leave him alone? He ain't doing nothing to you." "He's a sissy. Why don't you play us a song, sissy boy?" "Yeah, why don't you go back where you came from?" "Go get some macaroni, damn Eye-ties." "We was born here just like you." "But your mama, she don't speaka-da-inglish, does she?" Babe quickly puts his violin down and charges. He surprises me, and before I can set the shorties on the grass, one of the bojohns tackles me. I keep hold of the bag with one arm and try to break my fall with the other, but I feel the glass crunch under my belly as I land on the sidewalk. Damn. I smell the spilled whisky straight away, and my shirt and jacket are wet. The bojohn who tackled me relaxes for a second, and I pop him one on the side of the head with my free hand. Mrs. Tojetti runs out of her house, carrying her frying pan, yelling at the bojohns

17

to "Get the goddamn back to Orman where you belong." Mrs. Tojetti's a big woman, a real cozza, nobody mess with her, and the bojohns get up and start walking slow down Evans, looking back as us and laughing. "You boys okay? Frank, John?" I can smell the garlic over the whisky as she stands over me. I look over at Babe: he's already up and looking at his violin case. I sit up. "Thanks Mrs. Tojetti, we're okay. Three against two, you know?" "I know, I know." She starts lumbering back to her sausage. She turns around, gives me this big butta facia smile. "Hey Frank, you really oughtta stay offa the hooch." She laughs all the way up her walk.

I stand up. There's a little blood on my shirt, but mostly whisky. My jacket isn't too bad, except for my right sleeve, which is wet. The paper bag is at my feet, smashed and soaked. I'm afraid to look inside. I don't know what Secondino's going to do to me.

MOTHER

Oh dear. It doesn't smell very good here. The hospital smelled clean, like Mr. Clean, cotton and medicine, but it smells a little bit like Lakeview's cafeteria here, and a little like Jeff's dirty baby diapers. It looks nice and pretty. I like that shade of lavender on the walls and the shiny linoleum floors. And the nurses smile so. But it doesn't smell as good as it looks.

I don't know what's going to happen to me. I don't know if Ma will be able to find me here. That's not right. Something's not right with that. I don't know about the boys who used to come visit me and tell me nasty things and ask me to do nasty things. They didn't come to the hospital. I don't know, I get so confused lately, I don't know whether I'm coming or going. I wonder where my husband Joe is. Is he still alive? I can't remember. I like being in a wheelchair. I can walk. I like to walk. But I like the wheelchair. I'm a queen. "Mrs. DeShell? Frances? This is the television lounge and the dining room. This is where you'll eat your meals. Are you hungry now? Did you eat lunch at the hospital?" I don't remember. "Did you eat lunch at the hospital, dear?" I don't know. "No." "Are you hungry?" I nod. "After I show you your room, we'll see about getting you a snack. This is your room, Frances. Your roommate, Mrs. Robson, is asleep. She sleeps quite a bit. She doesn't talk, I'm afraid. But many of the other residents are quite friendly and chatty."

The room is small. There's not much furniture. I don't mind sharing. I enjoyed visiting with Mrs....oh, what was her name? Mrs. Something or other at the hospital. She told me all about her children, her grandchildren, her swollen ankles and the bad lungs she got from smoking. I was sorry when she left. It was so quiet. "This is your bed, Frances, and this is your nightstand. The closet on this side away from the window is for you. These two bottom drawers will be for your use. This is your sink, which you'll share with Mrs. Robson, and here is your bathroom, which you'll also share. There's a light above your bed here. Do you think you can remember all this, Frances? I know it's a lot." I nod again. "Sometimes it's hard to remember, isn't it? Why don't we make some signs to help? There are some cards on your bed, along with tape and a black magic marker. Why don't we make little tags to help you remember what things are? I'll sit down here on the chair, and we can use this table as a desk: see how it swings around over your wheelchair so it's like a little desk? Isn't that neat? There. Now take the magic marker in your hand, here...and let's write, CLOSET, that's good, C-L-O-S-E-T. Now LIGHT, L-I-G-H-T."

It's dark now, although I can see a shaft of light from the doorway. I wonder if they always keep the door open a crack. My bed is small, like the one in the hospital. I miss my big bed back at the house. I just bought a new mattress from Sears. A Beautyrest. I wonder when I can go home. I can hear a beep beep beep from the hallway. I can hear my roommate breathing softly in the corner

I'm thirsty. I didn't drink much water tonight because I don't want to wet myself in the bed. Joe would get so mad at me. He used to yell and yell every morning. I couldn't help it. I don't think anyone will yell at me here, but I don't want to cause anyone trouble, and I don't want to dirty the bedclothes. I never wet the bed when I was a little girl. My brother Lowell did when he was young. Up until the third grade. Ma wouldn't say a word, she'd just air the sheets out on the line before she washed them so that everyone could see the big yellow stains. He told Katie and Ira they were my sheets but everyone knew they were his. There was never any yelling at my house. It wasn't until I married Joe that I heard yelling like that.

I heard some yelling here after dinner. A tiny old man with one leg was eating at another table, and after dessert he started banging his cup with his spoon and yelling bad words. When I was in the hallway near the TV room I heard someone, it could have been him, yelling "help me, help me" over and over again. Poor little man. I wonder what happened to his leg.

My husband Joe came to visit after dinner. At least I think it was him. He gave me an ice cream cone and wheeled me around in the chair. He even took me outside by some rose bushes. I didn't say anything in case it wasn't really him. I don't want to be fooled. I'm not sure when he left. I might have fallen asleep. I didn't have a good feeling about him.

I don't have a good feeling about this place either. I don't know why they want to keep me here. I just want to go home. I like all the people, it's fun watching everyone go back and forth, and I like to listen to all the conversations, but something's not right. I wish I could remember what it was.

Something's not right. I should be able to remember better. Sometimes, I can't even think of the right word, or what I was going to say, or what I should say. So I nod, and smile, but it's not right. I'm not sure what's happening to me. Sometimes

21

I'm not even sure what day it is. Everyone has some trouble with their memory as they get older, I know that, but sometimes I can't remember what it is I've planned to say just a minute ago. I practice sometimes. When we went to Colorado Springs, when was it, a while ago, I practiced saying "I would like a Reuben sandwich please and an ice tea" in the car as we were driving up, but when we got to the restaurant I couldn't remember the words, and I couldn't say anything for a long time. The lady was waiting, she was nice about it, but I couldn't say anything. I was so embarrassed. Finally Joe ordered the sandwich for me. But I didn't get any ice tea. That's not right. Joe is sharp, and so are Jay and Ted. I can't remember anything anymore.

It's dark, and I can hear that lady breathing. I don't like that beeping. It makes it hard to go to sleep. I don't want to stay here. Maybe they'll help me get better, maybe they'll help me remember, and then they'll let me go home. Maybe I can go back to live with my mother and father. But I think that maybe my mother's dead. Oh dear.

My arm itches. The, what do you call those things, those hard things that they put your arm in when you hurt it, oh, I can't remember, anyway, my arm itches like the dickens. I'm tired. My arm itches and I have to go to the bathroom. I didn't drink anything all night, but I still have to go. I'm not used to being around so many people. I wish that beeping would stop.

FATHER

"Let me look at you." He's got a small scratch on his right cheek, but other than that, no black eye or nothing. His shorts have a grass stain near the belt on the right pocket. I brush some dry grass out of his hair. "You go home, wash up at the house before you go in. Say hi to Mama, but then go down to the room and wait for me. Don't tell nobody nothing." "Where are you going?" "I gotta see Mr. Secondino. Remember, don't say nothing." I haven't looked in the bag.

Three bottles, seventy-five cents. I don't know what Secondino's going to do, but I know he ain't going to forget it. No use waiting any longer. I kneel down and carefully, with my fingertips, open the bag and look inside. I see a bunch of broken glass, three big metal lids, but one of the lids is standing up. Yeah, one of the bottles looks okay. I take it gently out of the bag and hold it up to my face. It looks good, looks good. One bottle is better than none.

I want to take the other bottles, the broken ones, to Secondino too, so he don't think I stole 'em or nothing. The bag is wet and falling apart, so I wrap the broken glass as best I can, and press it against my belly with my left arm, while I carry the other bottle in my right. I hope I don't drop this other bottle. I don't want to walk up Box Elder, in case my father's home, so I walk down Elm and go around. Where's Mr. Big Shot now?

I finally get to Gagliano's garage, and I knock on the side door. Mr. Mastroantonio opens it. "Where you been, Frank?" "What's that smell? Has the kid been drinking? Ha ha." They're playing cards, the four of them, Mastroantonio with his white hair, Gagliano with his big belly and bushy mustachio, tall, stooped Cortese, who father calls "the question mark," and fat Secondino with his hair pomade and cheap suits. Everyone, except Mastroantonio, is smoking cigars. I can hear a baby crying somewhere in the house. "What happened kid?" Mastroantonio repeats. Secondino, who had been laughing and looking at his cards, gives me a quick glance and then back to his cards, "Hurry up kid, we're thirsty." I don't know what to do, so I keep standing there quiet in the doorway. "Giuseppe, it's your turn. Whattya going to do?" "I think I might like a drink before I decide." "Frankie! Come here goddamnit. What the hell's wrong with you?" I move slowly, and put the good bottle on the table. "That's one." Secondino is looking at me full now. "Where's two? Or tree?" I look down at my left arm, still holding the wet bag and broken glass. "They busted." "Whattya mean they busted? How'd they bust?" "Fight." "What? Did you say fight? Who'd you get in a fight with?" "My brother, some bojohns…" "You got in a fight with your brother? You were carrying *my* booze and you got in a fight with your brother?" Secondino stands up. "I oughtta knock the shit outta you." Cortese starts laughing and Gagliano says, "Calm down." He don't scare me. Maybe if he slaps me around, he'll forget about the two bits. "No, no, not *with* my brother. Some bojohns were ganging up on Babe, so I had to jump in. Two of the bottles got broke." "So you brought me the broken bottles, huh Frankie? Thanks." "Why don't you throw them in the garbage?" "I wanted you to see that I didn't steal 'em." "Why didn't you put the bottles down before you jumped in?" Mastroantonio asks, and pushes a garbage can toward me. I dump the bag and shake off my clothes. "I got surprised." "What happened Frankie?" "I get to Giarantano's no problem, and then I'm crossing Evans when I hear my brother calling. He's running up Evans, being chased by four or five bojohns. I ain't going to let my brother get stomped, so I run down Evans to meet him. We got jumped, until Mrs. Tojetti came out with a frying pan. Two of the shorties got broke. I saved the other one." "Oh, you saved one. Thank you Frankie, thank you very much. Listen, Frankie, what's your job? Tell me, what's your job?" "I ain't got no job. I'm in school." "No, after school, what's your job? When I gave you money today, what was your job?" "To get you three shorties from Giarantano's." "And to bring them back." "And to bring them back." "But you didn't do your job. When you saw your brother getting chased, whose time were you on?" I shrug my shoulders. "When you saw your brother getting chased, you were on *my* time. Not *your* time. *My* time. And so when you saw your brother getting chased up the street, you shoulda said to yourself, 'I gotta job to do. I ain't on my own time, otherwise I would help my brother. I'm on Secondino's time, and he's paying me to bring these shorties back. And that's what I need to do.' So because you goofed off on your job, two of my shorties got broke. The way I see it, you owe me for the tree shorties, plus the four bits for the bottles, plus another two bits. A buck fifty." "Leave the kid alone. He was helping his brother." "No one asked you, Mastroantonio. Buck fifty." "You charging the kid vig?" "Shut up." I hold the quarter out to him. "This is all I got." "Buck twenty-five." "I ain't got it." "You don't have a buck twenty-five? Then talk to your brother.

Your brother don't have it, then talk to your dad. Buck twenty-five, today. Now get the hell outta here."

I don't know what to do. How'm I going to get a buck twenty-five? I got maybe a nickel in my cigar box, and my father sure ain't going to jump at the chance to pay for Secondino's whisky. He's been quick with the belt since Mama got sick, and will probably give me a buck twenty-five whipping. I didn't hear no whistle, but from the smells of everyone's dinner cooking I can tell it must be late. I guess I should go home, although I ain't hungry no more. So much for the movies.

Ange is stirring the gravy and Jay is chopping something on the table as I walk in the back door. "Dad wants to see you." "You stink." "Is he mad?" "I don't know. He's downstairs." Babe must have told him. Damn.

I know he's down there waiting for me, but I walk lightly and slowly, trying not to creak the stairs. It doesn't work. "Hey, Frankie, is that you? I can smell you, you smell like a tavern. Get down here." He's sitting in his easy chair, and Connie is coloring on the floor. I can't tell if he's mad or not. "What happened? I hear you broke one of Secondino's shorties?" I tell him. He looks at me. "You fought for your brother. That's good. What does Secondino say?" "He says I owe him a buck twenty-five?" "A buck twenty-five? Mannaggia. That cheap cazzo." He leans back, takes a quarter from his pocket, and drops it into my palm. He takes out his money clip, peels off a dollar and holds it in front of me. He looks me in the eye. "You give this to him. But you owe me. You hear me, you owe me one dollar twenty-five. You hear?" I nod. He hands me the bill. He smiles. "Now go upstairs and clean up. And kiss Mama." I turn, surprised, relieved and happy. "Hey, booze. You ain't no Jack Dempsey. And don't forget, you owe me a buck and two bits."

26

MOTHER

They've taken me to a house exactly like our house. I don't know why. I don't know what they're going to do. I'm frightened. This chair is like the chair in our house. The lamp, the carpet, the couch. I can see patterns in the couch. Boys' faces. And trees. I don't know why I'm here. I don't know what I've done.

They're downstairs. A bunch of boys and the older one, Joe, my husband. My husband is going to leave me. He's going to leave me and get a new wife. He's told me so. He's going to leave me here with the boys and get a new wife, a new Italian wife, and have lots of children. So he can have grandchildren. Grandchildren and children and new Italian wives lined up around the block. And I'll be stuck here in this new house, looking out the window at all those people.

Someone is coming up the stairs. I'll pretend like I'm watching the news on TV. But the screen is dark, black. It's gone off and I don't remember how to turn it on. I'll close my eyes and pretend I'm sleeping. "Hello Frances. Open your eyes, we know you're awake." I open my eyes. Four boys are standing in front of me. One looks a little like Jeff, but the others all have red hair and freckles. They don't look exactly alike: they look more like brothers. They scare me.

One of the redheads speaks. "Can we see your underwear, Frances? Please?" I don't want to show them my underwear, but I'm frightened. I sit still and don't move. Sometimes they go away if I sit quiet. "Please, Frances, we want to see your underwear. If you don't show us your underwear, we'll tell you things. We tell you what Jeff has really been up to. Do you want to know what Jeff's been up to? Frances? Okay. He's been doing bad things. Lots of bad things. He doesn't have a job and he doesn't want one. All he wants to do is to smoke marijuana and screw girls. You know how he keeps moving around. That's because he keeps getting fired from those colleges for screwing all the girls. He doesn't tell you that does he? He doesn't tell you how many girls he screws and how he loves marijuana cigarettes. Sometimes he likes to puff on his marijuana cigarette while he screws a girl. That's why he doesn't have kids. Sometimes he even screws Mexican girls. Or black girls. He likes those the best."

That's not true. Jeff wouldn't do those things. You're lying.

"No Frances, I'm not lying. Let me show you how he does it." He moves toward me and puts his hand on my leg, next to my knee. I sit as quiet as a mouse. I can't see any of the other boys but I know they're there, watching. I can feel their hot breath on my shoulder. His hand feels cold on my leg. I don't like it. I close my eyes tight.

"First he puts his hand on the girl's leg. Then he bends down slowly, until he's on his knees, like this. Then he kisses the left knee." He kisses my knee with his dry lips. I shudder and keep my eyes closed tight. "Then he takes a puff of his marijuana cigarette, and kisses the other knee. You like this, don't you Frances." No, I don't like it. "Then he rubs the girls' legs. He starts down by the ankle and moves up with both hands. He moves up slowly, to get them all hot and bothered. First the knees, then higher. You're getting hot and bothered, aren't you Frances." I'm not getting hot and bothered. I want to scream or vomit. "When the girls are all hot and bothered from his hands rubbing up, not all the way up, he starts to kiss their legs on the inside of their thighs, barely above the knees. Like this. Oh Frances. You are getting hot and bothered, aren't you? You might as well admit it. We're not going to tell. You like this, don't you?"

I do not like this. I'm having a hard time breathing. Why are you doing this to me? I haven't done anything to you. Why are you hurting me like this?

"I'm not hurting you Frances. I'm just kissing you, and showing how your son screws every girl he sees. You like to be kissed, admit it. You used to like to be kissed very much." I don't like to be kissed anymore. I'm old. Leave me alone.

"After he gets the girls all hot and bothered by rubbing and kissing their legs, he likes to have a look up there. It's usually dark up there, so he needs some light. Do you know what he uses for a light, Frances? Do you know what he uses to look all the way up there? A lamp. A simple living room lamp. Like this." I can feel heat on my legs. I open my eyes and see the boy on his knees with one of the living room lamps in his hand. It looks just like the one at home. He's taken off the shade and is smoking a cigarette and holding the lamp between my knees. I want to cross my legs but I'm afraid he'll burn me with the bulb. He takes a puff on his cigarette and leans over so that I can only see the lamp and the top of his red head. I can feel the heat from the lamp and my stomach feels queasy. I close my eyes and try to think of nice things like birds and trees and flowers but I can't. The room begins to spin and spin.

I open my eyes. The boys have gone. I'm alone. The lamps are on the end tables. Everything looks like our house but I know that it's not. The telephone is ringing. I get up and answer it.

"Hello."

"Hi Mom, it's Jeffrey, your son."

I don't want to talk.

MOTHER

FATHER

Damn it's hot. I can taste the dust in my mouth. What else is new? Me and Babe are skipping school today to see President Roosevelt down at the depot. I'm glad it's Thursday, so I can wear my ROTC uniform. Saves on clothes, saves on clothes. I like the way I look in my uniform, handsome, like I know what I'm doing. The girls, they like what they see. I ain't no football player, but I know how to handle a gun, if you know what I mean. Too bad I won't see Donna D'Antonio today. Marone she's got the breasts, I get a hard on just thinking about her.

We're meeting by the boy's gym. He's supposed to be here by now. I'm going to skip Shop, Biology and Civics, and Babe's gotta miss History, English and Orchestra. He don't like to miss History, but I said, "Babe, this *is* history," so that decided him. Duck soup. He ain't never seen a president before. My father took me to see Roosevelt a couple of years ago. My father likes Roosevelt, says he's for the little people. I want to ask him if we're going to get in a war. I hope Babe left his violin at home. A couple of my buddies, Sal Diadosa, John Gonzalez and fat Marty DeLuca are probably already down there, checking out the birds. I'd really like to get with Donna D'Antonio. I don't think she's seeing anybody. I hear she lives clear on North Erie, across the tracks. Hey Donna I gotta da pork chop, hey Donna I gotta da lamb chop. I wouldn't mind getting into her flopper stoppers: I'd be her butcher boy. There's Ginny Delvecchio, a friend of Jay's. Always over the house, but don't even say hi to me at school. Stuck up Ginny. Butta facia. Thick cheaters too. Jeepers, Creepers, ain't you got no peepers. Where the hell is my brother?

There he is. And he's got his violin. Jesus. I ain't going to help him carry it. "Hey, Sergeant York." "About time. Where you been? Why'd you bring your violin, Jasper?" "I thought maybe I'd make it back in time for practice." "You ain't gonna make it back in time for practice. C'mon, let's go." "What's your hurry, Frank? We only have to walk down Broadway, then Union for a couple of blocks. We got an hour." "I got two bits and I thought we could stop at the Broadway Drugstore and get us a couple of cokes. You hungry?" "I could eat. We could split a hamburger or something." "There's Maria Piserchio. She's got nice pins." "She's from hunger. A bunch of calico." "What do you know about it?" I punch him in the arm. "What do you know about the cuzz?" "I know as much as you." "You know as much as I do? You know nothing." We start to walk down the hill, through the baseball field and off the schoolyard.

As we pass the library, I can see a big crowd across the bridge. I just had a coke at the drugstore, and my mouth is already dry again. That Mr. McFarland, he didn't like us splitting a hamburger, especially when Babe asked for some more bread to go with it. "Why aren't you kids in school?" he said. "They let us out to see the president," Babe answered. "Civics and History and stuff. Can I have some more bread?" My brother's got a smart mouth on him, I thought McFarland was gonna smack him one. Babe likes his bread. Just like my father.

The wind's picking up. A straw hat flies off a hoosier's head in front of me and off the bridge. It was really hot a couple of years ago. And dry. We had to drag a chain from the back axle of the Oldsmobile so static electricity wouldn't short out the battery. I see a couple of broads wearing those old dust masks from three, four years ago. Show-offs. We wore gas masks once in ROTC: mine stunk so bad I could hardly breathe.

The guy's looking for his hat over the railing, and I look too. Corona's pretty much abandoned. They cleaned it up pretty good. Three years ago, Babe and I would fill our wagon with Giarantano's wine and head down to Corona, where everyone was living in tents, shacks and abandoned cars, cooking on campfires and washing in the Arkansas or the creek. These weren't bums and hobos neither, but real people, families and kids. The city and the mill put up a few outhouses, but it still stunk, and you still had to watch where you stepped. Giarantano told us never to take no trades: cash only cash only. They was always trying to barter with us: a dozen apples, a pitchfork, a can of gasoline, paint your fence—we ain't got no fence, mister—a car tire. One time this old guy even wanted to trade his mutt for a jug. That mutt was older than he was, wouldn'ta lasted a week. "Hey Babe, remember when that old guy wanted to trade his dog for a jug of wine? That dog was older'n he was." "Yeah, I remember. I liked that dog. I felt sorry for it. They both looked like they hadn't eaten for a month. I brought a sandwich for them the next day, but they were gone." "You brought them a sandwich, huh? I didn't know that." "Yeah, but I couldn't find them, so I had to eat it myself."

33

The Union Avenue Bridge is full of people. This gray Cord Westchester slowly tries to cross the bridge, but there are too many people, so it has to stop. I elbow Babe. "What a strunze. That's a nice car though. I'm going to get me a car like that, and the broads will be all over me. Donna D'Antonio, Julie McBride, Maria Piserchio, even Ginny Delvecchio, they'll all be doing the boogie-woogie in my back seat: Ti-pi-ti-pi-ton ti-pi-ton, I'll keep on stealing till I get that feeling, till I get satisfied." "That's not how it goes." "That's how it's gonna go with me. Ti-pi-ti-pi-ton ti-pi-ton."

We cross the bridge and veer left, toward the depot. The crowd is milling northwest, so we keep walking. Except for a few slobs, people are dressed up, men in suits and ties, women in dresses, even though it feels like ninety. And almost everyone in hats. That's good, shows Pueblo has respect. I see a couple of doughboys in uniform. Looking good, looking good. I hope people think I'm a real soldier. I ask Babe if my sidecap's straight. Damn it's hot. That sun, it don't stop.

MOTHER

"C'mon Frances, you're going to be late." I am not going to be late. I have almost an hour and a half. Joe gets so
nervous; you'd think he was going to fly instead of me. I like
to fly, although it scares me a little. I like the food. I'm flying to
Pennsylvania to see my son Jeff and his wife Lisa.

He's way up the steps, and he turns around and gives
me that hateful look, his face all scrunched up like a hateful
old man. He looks like a bum in his frayed brown sports coat,
thin cotton shirt and maroon pants. I hope I look nice. It took
me a long time to dress. Even though I put my nice dress with
the blue and purple flowers out last night, when I got up this
morning I just couldn't remember where I put my stockings. I
looked and looked and finally found them in the desk drawer
where I keep the bills. I'm getting forgetful.

I hope I look nice. I hope this sweater isn't too old fash-
ioned. Sometimes I get cold on airplanes. Or at least I did last
year. Look at that, a man talking into a little telephone. It looks
like he's talking into his hand. There's another one. It looks like
they are all talking into their hands. Maybe they're all talking to
each other. How funny.

They had an escalator at Joslin's Department store. The
old one downtown. I enjoyed shopping there but they were too

expensive. I don't like the new store at the mall.

This airport is shiny and new. We had some trouble finding it, and Joe had to ask a man at the gas station for directions. It turned out that we were on the right road to begin with, and just hadn't gone far enough. Joe gets so crabby sometimes.

There's a baby in a carriage coming down the other side. Don't sit under the apple tree with anyone else but me. Maybe Jeff and Lisa will have a baby someday. That would be nice. The baby is so cute. A cute little Mexican baby.

I'm falling.

It's funny, all the people looking down at me like that. Where's Joe, my husband? "Are you okay, lady?" I think I am. Nothing really hurts. "Frances! Frances! What happened? What have you done? What have you done?" That's my husband, Joe. He usually doesn't sound like that. His voice is higher, thinner or something. "Don't try to move, lady. Someone should call an ambulance." "Frances, can you hear me?" "Yes, Joe, I can hear you. Everyone at the airport can hear you." People laugh. "Try sitting up. Can you sit up?" "I think so." I twist over on my side and Joe helps me sit up. I can't see very well. Everything is cloudy. "Here are her glasses." Someone puts them over my face. There, that's better. I straighten them up. I feel strange, funny, surprised, but nothing really hurts. "Do you need some water? Get her some water." "Is there a doctor around?" A young man sits down on the floor next to me. He has a neatly trimmed beard and long hair tied back. "What's your name?" I look at him. He has a kind face. "You're Frances, right?" I nod. "Can you move, Frances?" I nod again. "Does anything hurt?" I shake my head no. "Would you like to try to stand up?" The floor is getting uncomfortable. "Yes." He springs to his feet. "Let's get you up. Sir, would you take her other arm?" He takes

36

my elbow on one side and Joe takes the other, and they help me up. I'm fine. Not dizzy at all.

I notice that one of my shoes is gone. I look down and see that I've ripped my stocking on the other leg, and I have a couple of small cuts on that ankle. Darn! I want to look pretty to see my son. Is he here? No, no, he's in Pennsylvania. I have to fly on an airplane to see him.

A young girl hands me a bottle of water. The young man in the ponytail takes the bottle, opens the top and hands it to me. "Can you drink?" The water is cold. I don't like drinking from plastic bottles and a little drips down my chin. Joe dabs my chin with his handkerchief. He looks nervous. I notice a smear of lipstick on the plastic. I must look a fright. I touch my hair to see if it's still in place. "Would you like to sit down? Let's move over to these chairs and sit down." "Goddamn city and their goddamn buildings. Who'd build an escalator like that? Who'd build an escalator like that with all these people?" The nice young man takes the bottle from me and gently leads me over to one of the chairs. I walk funny because I've only got one shoe. "Where's her other shoe?" I sit down and the nice young man sits down next to me. "Does she need a doctor?" "I don't think so." The rest of the people go away except two women. One is about Jeff's age and the other is younger, maybe about twenty. "We should call an ambulance or something. God damn it Frances! This is a faulty escalator. I'll sue the goddamn city of Colorado Springs." "Look at me, please, Frances." I look at him. He takes my glasses off and looks me straight in the eyes. "We should call an ambulance. I'll sue the goddamn city." "Does anything hurt Frances?" "No." He moves his head slowly to the side, still looking into my eyes. "I think you're okay. Yes, I think you're fine. Maybe a bit shaken up, but otherwise fine." He turns his head. "She doesn't have

37

a concussion, and nothing else seems to be hurt or bruised. It seems like she's walking okay. I saw her fall, and her rump took most of the impact. You can call an ambulance if you want, but I think she'll be fine. If she starts hurting, she should probably see a doctor, but it doesn't seem like anything's bothering her now." "I've got her shoe." A little blond boy of about ten holds out my shoe. I take it. "Do you want to put your shoe on Frances? What time is her plane?" "Eleven." "You've got plenty of time. My girlfriend, Sarah, will take her to the restroom and get her cleaned up a bit. She'll check her out a little, she's a nurse as well." "Thank you. Thank you very much." "She's a fine lady. Frances, this is Sarah. She'll take you to the restroom where you can wash your face and change stockings. Whenever you're ready."

FATHER

I'm going out with Donna D'Antonio this afternoon. A double feature at the Chief Theater: Douglas Fairbanks Jr. in *Party Girl* and then Edward G. Robinson in *Little Caesar*. I've already seen *Little Caesar*, but it's a good picture. This is Rico speaking, Rico, R-I-C-O, Little Caesar, that's who. I got almost a whole dollar, and five dog food labels too, so she can get in for free. We'll have us some cokes, some popcorn, and I'll get a little balcony action. I hope *Party Girl* is first, get her warmed up. I got my Arrow shirt, my good blazer and slacks, my two-tone bucks that cost my father three dollars at Montgomery Ward. And my felt fedora. It's hot, but I'll still wear a tie. Ten cents a dance, that's what they pay me, gosh how they weigh me down. A little Aqua Velva...damn, I look nice.

What time is it? Almost one thirty. I'm supposed to meet Donna at the theater at a quarter after two. The newsreels start at two thirty. I got a little time. I think Ange is doing the ironing, maybe I'll ask her to give my tie a quick one-two.

"Hey Ange. You got time to give my tie a quick one-two?" "C'mon. Don't be like that." "Just a quick one-two." "Thanks." "Pa's looking for me, huh?" "What's he want?" "Well, you ain't seen me, okay?" "I'm going to the pictures with Donna." "I'll be back in time for dinner."

The tie's hot in my fingers, and I have some trouble getting it right. There we go, perfect. It looks good, crisp. I'd better get going. I'll go out the back, in case my father's in the living room. One last glance in the mirror, and I'm off.

"What?" "I'm in here." "I'm going to the movies." "What?" "Okay, I'm coming." Damn. I don't know what he wants. He probably wants me to go to the store or something. I should have left, goddamn it, I should have left. "I'm coming, I'm coming."

He's standing by the front door, putting on his cap and jacket in the mirror. He turns and gives me the once over. I don't feel good about this. "Where you going all dressed up?" "I'm going to the pictures with Donna. A double feature at the Chief." "You're going to the pictures, huh?" He turns back to the mirror and adjusts his cap. He don't say nothing. I stand there waiting. I hear some moke grind his gears in the street outside. My father opens the door and stands in the frame. "Come here." I walk to stand behind him. I think he's going to tell me about cars and gears and stuff. "You see the grass?" "Yeah, I see it." "It needs mowing." "I'll do it when I get back." "You'll do it now." "I'm going to the pictures, I got a date." "Whatdya say? I'm not going to tell you twice." "Why can't I do it when I get back?" "Because I said you'll do it now. Don't talk back to me." "I'm not talking back, but I made plans." He turns and backhands me hard in the face. "Ow. I'm not talking back. I'm not talking back." "The next one I close my fist." "Okay, I'll do it. I'll mow the grass. Yes sir, I'll mow the grass." He steps out the door. "I'll be home by four. The grass will be mowed by then."

Goddamn son of a bitching fuck. Fucking fuck goddamn. I got to mow the grass. I had a date, I had plans, and he wants me to mow the grass. Nothing ever works out for me, nothing ever works out. I hate my fucking father, I hate my fucking father. I was gonna get some action this afternoon, I was gonna get some action, but now I gotta mow the goddamn fucking son of a bitch cocksucking grass. Look at it, it looks like a fucking jungle out there. Goddamn motherfuck it to hell. I slam the door so hard, the Saint Joseph's statue on the windowsill falls off. Fuck fuck fuck. I bend down to look at it. Lucky it didn't break. Thank God for small favors. I leave it on the floor.

I hate this fucking life. My father's been quick with the fists since my mother died, quick with the fists. I need to get the fuck out of here, move out on my own. Six more months I'm out of high school, and I'm gone. See ya later alligator. I should just go to the movies, I should just go, tell him to go fuck himself. He'd clean my clock, but it'd be worth it. God, I hate his fucking guts.

I gotta change my clothes. Donna's going to be sore at me, but what can I do? I ain't going to go all the way to Santini's drug store to the telephone. She ain't got a phone anyway. Fuck my father fuck my father fuck my father. I stomp up the stairs, making as much noise as possible. One of my sisters has left a basket of laundry on the landing in front of our bedroom door, and I give it a good kick. That feels so good I kick it again.

"What do you care what I'm doing? Leave me alone, Jay, leave me alone." "I can't wait to get out of here, I can't wait to get out of this fucking house." "Pa, that's why. Our fucking father." "I don't care, I'll talk like I want to talk." "He hasn't earned my respect, he hasn't earned my respect." "I was gonna go to the pictures, a double feature at the Chief with Donna, but he wants me to mow the grass." "It can't wait, it's gotta be done now. By the time he gets back." "I don't know why. Ask him." "He just wants to fuck me up." "Because he's fucking mean, that's why. He just wants to fuck me up." I go inside our room and slam the door. I feel like smashing something. God I feel like smashing something.

I sit on the bed and take off my shoes, left, right, without unlacing them and throw them on the floor. This is a hard fucking life, a hard fucking life. "GOD DAMN IT GOD DAMN IT GOD DAMN IT." I twist around and punch the pillow two or three times. I hate my fucking father. I hate my fucking life. I hear a noise outside, and get up to look out the window. I see my sister Ange watching my sister Jay pushing the lawnmower.

I put my shoes back on.

FATHER

MOTHER

"I'm going sixty miles an hour and everyone's passing us like we're standing still. Go you bastards, go. I don't know why they had to change the speed limit back to seventy-five. Where's everyone going? Huh Frances? Where's everyone got to go? Frances? Answer me!"

"I don't know, Joe, I don't know." He's in a good mood today. I'm surprised. He didn't even scream and holler when I forgot to make his orange juice this morning. He's usually crabby when we drive up to Colorado Springs to put the money in the bank. Like he'd rather be going alone. But today he's nice. I wonder how long it will last.

I like going to Colorado Springs. I like going anywhere. I like coming back, too, because then I'm on the side where the mountains are. We'll go downtown to deposit the money, because Joe insists that if we put it in a Colorado Springs bank we won't spend it as easily, then we'll go eat somewhere, either the Village Inn, the Olive Branch, or the Broadmoor. I hope we go to the Broadmoor. It's a little bit more expensive, but the atmosphere is much nicer. I like the heavy silverware that has the Broadmoor design on it, and the nice white cloth napkins. The French Dip sandwich has good roast beef, and you get a big salad that comes with it. We have a Broadmoor credit card.

The traffic does seem fast. I'm glad I'm not driving. I don't like driving that much anymore. Especially when I'm not sure where I'm going. Sometimes, even when I know where I'm going, I forget how to get there and make a wrong turn or go past where I'm supposed to stop. I guess I'm getting old.

I'm getting sleepy. Joe has the heat on, and the sun is warm on my side of the car. Joe's got a Mexican station loud on the radio. I don't mind, it sounds lively. It's so bright outside. The sun is really beating down. We had six inches of snow, but most of it is melting and turning the ground to mud. There's a train running the opposite direction parallel to the highway. I can see cattle cars, but they go by too fast to see if they're full or empty. There's a big sign for Santa's Workshop at the North Pole. Aunt Virginia and I took Jeff there once. He had fun. He liked riding that little train around the workshop. Virginia was always good for that sort of thing. There's a small sign for the Red Rooster Bar and Grill. Oh, the signs are set up like those old Burma Shave signs. I remember driving in that old Studebaker with my brother in Illinois, and we crossed the bridge into Missouri. And we saw Riot at/Drug store/Calling all cars/100 customers/99 jars. And we laughed and laughed. And we were going to the drug store, to get some shaving cream for my father, but since the sign said they were all out, we turned around. I hoped dad wouldn't be angry. "Frances, wake up! We're almost at the bank, we're almost at the bank."

It's windy. I just had my hair fixed; I hope the wind doesn't mess it all up. There aren't too many people about. "C'mon Frances, c'mon." I know I'm slow. I'm not in any hurry. We cross the street at the light, and walk down the sidewalk into the bank. He charges ahead to the island where the deposits slips are. I see a big cardboard Easter bunny with a basket full of money. That's cute. The bank isn't very crowded. I see about seven or eight customers and fifteen or so tellers, managers, and the like. "C'mon Frances, c'mon. I'm waiting. I'm waiting." I walk over to the island. I hate this part. He does this every time. It makes me so nervous. "Do you have your check, Frances, do you have your check?" I set my purse on the counter, and rummage around, looking for the long envelope with the check inside. I hope I didn't forget it. "Frances! Do you have the check, Frances?" He's so loud, and I know people are looking at him. At us. I see the envelope and look inside. Thank God the check is there. "Here it is." "Take a deposit slip. Here. Here. And write your account number. Five six six seven eight two. C'mon Frances. Five six six seven eight two. Five six six seven eight two. Don't make your fives like that. Write nice goddamn it! Okay. Now put one thousand dollars in that box. One thousand dollars. There. There! Now the date. The date, Frances, the date. Okay. Now sign it. You do this on purpose. You burn me up. Okay, let's take it to the teller." This is such an ordeal. He makes me so nervous, I can hardly think straight.

"Can I help you?" And now he's going to start in on the teller. He thinks he's being smart. "Yes. We'd like to deposit this money into our savings passbook account. But I have a question. Why is it that we're only making two and a half percent, but that you charge twelve and even twenty percent for loans and credit cards? We have over fifty thousand dollars in your bank, and we're not making any interest." "The two and a half percent is what our passbook pays. Almost all banks pay the same. Would you like to speak to an investment counselor? We offer many investment opportunities besides low yield simple interest savings accounts." "No. I just want to know why you don't pay any more interest. We have over

45

fifty thousand dollars in your bank." "As I've tried to explain, sir, our current passbook rate is two and a half percent. We do have other investment opportunities. Would you like to speak to someone about them?" "No." She's pretty, a pretty Hispanic woman. "Would you like anything else?" "No." "Okay, here's your receipt, and this is your balance. Have a good day." Joe takes the receipt and walks away. I smile at the girl and follow.

I'm going to have to go to the bathroom soon. I went just before we left, but it's been a while. I can wait until we get to the restaurant though. I'm hungry. "Frances! Let's sit down here for a minute. Here. Let's sit down." Why does he want to sit down here, in the lobby of the bank? "Frances, sit down." I sit down next to him. He yawns. "Two and a half percent interest. Highway robbery." He picks up a money magazine and begins to leaf through it. I'd like a drink of water. A tall man in a dark suit man comes over to us from his desk. "Hello there. How may I help you?" Joe looks up from his magazine. "Yes, sir, uh, I have a question. Why is it that we're making two and a half percent interest on our savings account, but the bank can charge up to twenty percent for loans? Why is that?" "Are you a customer of the bank sir?" "Am I a customer? Of course I'm a customer. What do you think I'm doing here? I'm a big customer with substantial savings in your bank. You can ask Mr. Herrera if a Mr. DeShell is a customer of your bank. And I just want to know, how come you can pay two and a half percent to savings accounts while charging twenty percent interest on loans? That's all I'm asking." "I'm sorry sir, I didn't mean to offend you. We do pay two and a half percent on passbook savings, but I don't think we charge twenty percent for anything, except maybe some very risky loans. Which we don't make anyway. If you'd like to speak to an investment counselor or a financial services advisor to get your money into more productive venues, I'm sure we could get you in right now." "No. Thank you." "Is there anything I can help you with?" "No."

After a while, Joe yawns again and stands. "Let's go Frances. Let's go to the Broadmoor."

FATHER

It's always fucking freezing in this crate. I'm glad I'm wearing my monkey suit. It's bulky but it's warm. I always forget how cold it gets up here. I would not want to be in the nose or the stinger. Might as well paint a big bull's-eye on your chest. And that mulignan in the belly: no room for his parachute, he's gotta climb out of that death hole before he can put his chute on. It's not like we're going see any Kraut planes up here anyway. And Pennyman on my ass. Always checking up on me. Calls me Guiseppe, the motherfucking Anglo. Guiseppe. You teach him good, Guiseppe, you teach him good. Kiss my ass, you Yankee Anglo. All, or nothing at all. All or nothing at all.

I got this stupid cracker from Mississippi wondering what end of the gun to shoot. Derrick. "Hold on, hold on: he's just feathering the engines. Nothing to worry about., nothing to worry about." Gonzalez's chicken almost jumped out of his skin. "Hey Gonzalez, your chicken's got buck fever. Better hold his hand before he messes his drawers." "Your electric suit working?" "Don't call me sir, I'm a sergeant." "These suits will keep you nice and toasty, nice and toasty. It's heavy, but think about freezing your ass off without it." "We've been up here holding our dicks for a while, so the captain'll tell us to test the fifties soon. And then, while he's climbing, we'll try on our flak jackets and hit the oxygen. We'll level off, test the guns again, do a couple of fire drills. You listen to what I say and you'll be all right. After the fire drills we'll probably do a couple of dry runs over the range before we do our real run. We've got live general purpose ordnance. This is your first run, so I should warn you, there's a lot of waiting up here. Lot of standing around. Don't let Pennyman catch you sitting down, it'll be both our asses."

I don't know what the fuck I'm doing up here. Keep 'em flying is our battle cry, do your part for duty, honor, country. Flying out of Westover beats flying out of Guadalcanal. I couldn't take the jungle. The heat and the bugs. I spent a couple of months in Louisiana, first at Barksdale and then at Esler Air Field near Alexandria, and I thought I was going to die. I wouldn't mind going to Europe, but they won't send us wops west. My brother might be sent east, after he finishes officers' school at Fort Benning. I wish I was down on the ground in Boston, getting some skirt. These eastern dames can be cold, but once you turn their motor over, watch out. Or back in Pueblo, hanging around with Tommy the Rock and JoJo at Gus' or Coors Tavern, drinking beer and chasing broads. Eating my sisters' spaghetti. If there is love, there is no in-between. I don't need love, I need to get in between some legs. I got one thing on my mind, one thing on my mind. I had what, not even two years between high school and basic training. Motherfuckers were on me as soon as I turned twenty-one. Order to Report for Induction, from the President of the United States. Sent July 6th, 1942. Report July 23rd.

"You've been shooting on the range, right? And they taught you how to load, how to sight, and how to get the gun unjammed, right? And every six rounds is a tracer? We've got live ammo up here, so don't screw around and shoot our wing off. Stand up here and take the gun. There. Watch it, watch it. I'll tell you when to fire. A short burst. You've got limited ammo, so don't go wild. Keep calm. You don't want to blow your wad on the first Messerschmitt you see. A short burst, short burst." "We'll wait until the captain gives us the go-ahead. He's a first louie, but a-ok. That's cold turkey."

"Roger." "Hang on, we gotta dive. Someone thinks they saw a German sub off Newport. Hang on to that handle there. There. If you need to barf, use that sack over there. Don't stick your head out the window, it'll come back in your face."

"See anything? I don't see anything." We're about five hundred feet, descending over a bay. We bank left over this big island, and there's another big island in front of us. There's a bunch of ships, tugboats and even a couple of sailboats scattered throughout. Mostly civilian. There's a few PT's over there but nothing heavy. Everything's slow and lazy. Nobody seems too bothered by the sub sighting. War seems far away. We level off at about one fifty-two hundred feet. I get this quick picture of a little town with a couple of fishing boats moored to a pier and a boy in short pants falling off a bicycle and then it's green forest and we're over water again with an island or what you call them peninsula in the distance. It's pretty up here: the blue water and the green land. I'm getting hot. I switch off my monkey suit and unzip my flight jacket. We should probably put our flak jackets on if we're going to engage. "Switch off your suit. I said, switch off your suit." I go to the locker and hand out the flak jackets to Gonzalez, his chicken, my chicken and then put on one myself. The jacket feels good to me.

We bank left and I hold the fifty to steady myself. We're about treetop level, angling out away from shore. This is probably a goose chase, but at least it's warmer down here. And we

don't need oxygen. Those masks make me gag. And if I fell under the spell of your call, I would be, caught in the undertow.
I could use some shut-eye. Maybe I'll take a nap when we get
back to base. A shower and a nap.

I hear Simon, the Negro bellygunner, yelling, "Two
o'clock, two o'clock" at the captain. That's Gonzalez's side.
My chicken starts over there. "Stay there, soldier. Man your
post!" I undo the safety of the fifty as we bank right. Gonzalez says he sees it, and I can hear the bomb bay doors grind
open. We ain't carrying depth charges, so we'll have to bomb
the fucker. My first action. We straighten up and level off at
under a hundred. I hear the order for a gun test, and fire a
short burst into the sea. We cruise along for a while. The captain asks if anybody sees anything. I don't see nothing except
the water. Did we lose it? Jacobson, the nose gunner's yelling,
"Straight ahead straight ahead." I hear him firing. Simon starts
firing too. We bank left and climb, and I hear Gonzalez open
up with his fifty. Then everyone stops and we level off. It's
quiet except for the engines. Then Simon and Jacobson start
firing again. The plane lurches and rises as the bombs go, and
almost immediately I hear the explosions behind me. We bank
left again and climb to circle back. Simon's yelling "We got it
we got it." I see nothing but the sky. We level off and I do see
something down below, a dark circle on the blue sea. Must
be the oil slick. It looks almost reddish. The captain says we
got something but let's take another look. McFadden, the tail
gunner, says, in that slow voice, "That ain't a sub: we killed
ourselves a whale." We drop a little and bank right, and I get
the full view. I see black chunks of whale floating in a bright
red pool of blood. We killed ourselves a whale. We keep bank-
ing, then climb to go back to base. No one says anything. How
stupid we are.

"A careless word, a needless sinking," McFadden says, and begins to laugh. Pennyman tells him shut it quick, but Gonzalez chimes in with "Our planes can take it, and dish it out." We're all cracking up, even Pennyman I think. "You know, captain, fish is a fighting food." I crank the safety back on the fifty. We killed ourselves a whale.

MOTHER

"Turn left, past those two trees. You can park there, over by that old truck." "It looks pretty deserted, Mom." "I know. It looked like this when I came out last time. You have to ring that buzzer over there by the gate, and if they're home, or if they feel like it, they let you in. I'm so mad. They said they would take care of it forever, and look at it now. Look at all those tumbleweeds and everything. And all those rusted tools. It's a shame."

"Did you ring?" "I pressed the buzzer twice. I think they're home, they're just not answering." "This happened the last time I was here. Your dad wanted to have him cremated, but I wanted someplace we could visit him. This was nice when I buried him here, with grass and everything. But now it's just tumbleweeds and old junk." "I think I see someone over there by the stables. You press the buzzer, and I'll go around and see if I can find someone."

I press the buzzer again. I want Jeff to see where his dog is buried. I don't even recognize anything here. They really let things go. This wasn't cheap. It would have been cheaper to have cremated him. I trusted that woman. She promised me they would take care of the grave as long as they owned the property. And that we could visit any time. She lied to me.

The wind's whipping up and it's getting chilly. We should have started out earlier. I'm glad I wore my gloves.

"We're closed!" "We would like to visit my dog, Star. I buried him here a year and a half ago. With Mrs. Helprin." "I'm sorry lady, but we're closed." "But when can I see him? Last time I came no one was here." "We don't really run that business anymore. Maybe if you call first, we could make some arrangement." "But Mrs. Helprin said…" "Sorry." He turns away and walks back toward the house. I wonder if he's Mrs. Helprin's husband. I never should have trusted her. I guess we should go. We could call, and try to come back tomorrow.

"Is he going to open the gate?" "No. He said we could call. Maybe we'd better go." "Fuck him. Sorry Mom. There's another gate over there on the side. We could go in that way." "Do you think we should? Won't they get mad?" "What are they going to do? You said they told you we could visit any-time. Besides, we're just going to look: we'll stay five minutes and then we'll go. C'mon Mom, this way, there's a little trail here."

I'm not sure this is a good idea. This is their property. The man said they don't run that business anymore. What does that mean? He was such a good little dog. He got snappy though as he got older. Joe treated him terribly at the beginning. He would pin his arms back on the floor until he screamed. But then he got used to him I guess. They got used to each other. He would take him for walks almost every day. And Star would always look to Joe for a treat. It's funny how dogs learn habits. I don't care for Jeff's dogs as much as I cared for Star.

"The gate's unlocked. We'll just stay five minutes. It'll be okay." Jeff knows about things more than I do. I'm a little nervous. He opens the gate and walks right through. I follow. I hear dogs barking near the house. "Watch out for that dog

54

shit Mom. Do you remember where he's buried?" I hesitate, and look around. I never used this gate before, and everything is so different. It used to be a nice lawn, and now its just dead grass with bare patches of dirt. We're standing on the bottom of a path that runs up a little hill to the other gate. I remember that skinny tree over there by the corner of the fence: I think the animals are buried in two rows between that tree and the gate. There's a heap of old machinery to the right of the gate, which didn't used to be there, and a bunch of tumbleweeds blown against the fence near the tree. The wind is picking up. The tree shakes, and another tumbleweed blows against the fence. "I think he's buried up there by that tree. But I can't be sure. Everything looks so different." "Let's go check it out." Jeff takes my elbow and helps me up the little hill.

We reach the top of the hill and I look left toward the tree. From the path to the tree, the ground has been paved over with gray concrete. I can't believe it. I look down and see markings in the concrete. I think Star is buried closer to the fence. Because of the way the hill slopes, I have to walk on the concrete to get closer to the tree. The pavement is rough, and Jeff takes my arm. "It was such nice grass, and they paved it all over. I can't believe it." "Maybe you can get your money back." Jeff kneels down. "Here he is." I kneel down too. I hope I can get up. The cement is rough on my knees. They've stenciled the name 'Star' in cursive with blue paint, which is already chipped and faded. That's the only way to tell he's here, underneath the pavement. I'm just sick.

"Hey! What are you doing out there? I told you we was closed!" "We're not bothering you. We're just looking at my dog." "This is private property." Jeff helps me to my feet. "Are you okay Mom?" "I suppose so. I'm just sick about this. It was such a nice place, and Mrs. Helprin promised they were going to take care of it." "Is Mrs. Helprin here?" "What?" "Is Mrs. Helprin here?" "She's busy." "The sooner we talk to Mrs. Helprin, the sooner we leave." "See them dogs over there?" He points to a chain link pen near the gate with the buzzer. I can see dark shapes and hear barking. "The live ones? I think you'd better leave now." Jeff doesn't say anything for a while. I don't want to cause any more trouble. I just want to go home. He turns to me. "What do you want to do, Mom?" "We'd better go." Jeff mutters a bad name under his breath.

As we turn to go, I see Mrs. Helprin walk out of the house and stand behind the man. I'm sick about this. "Do you remember me, Mrs. Helprin? I'm Mrs. DeShell. I buried our dog, Star, out here a year and a half ago. You said you'd take care of it, Mrs. Helprin. You said you'd take care of it."

She doesn't say anything. She just looks at me, and then turns and walks back into the house.

We walk down the hill and out the gate to the car.

FATHER

What do I say to you? My father. My old man. What do I say to you, lying there helpless, drugged with morphine and ninety pounds from the cancer, sheets yellow from sweat even though it's December, hands clawing into the mattress? What do I say to you? "How you doing?" "Thank you?" "I'm sorry?" "Goodbye?"

My old man. Not that old. Fifty-five. Came over alone when you were sixteen. All the way from Napoli to New York. Sixteen years old. No English, took the train from New York to Pueblo, worked in the CF & I for forty years. They changed your name, the bastards. They couldn't pronounce it. Fruscella. DeShell. DeShell. Sounds French. Anglo bastards. Fathered eight children, raised six. Two died, Louis at birth and little Joe at a year and a half. Influenza. My mother passed when you were forty-two. Your wife. I was twelve. Just before the Depression. You raised us all through the Depression, and the four girls through the war. And now this.

Your hands. Jesus God how thin and weak they look now. You could fix anything with those hands. You were eighteen when they took you off the shovels at the furnaces and had you try to repair one of the machines. You fixed everything they had. You must have been happy not to work the furnaces.

57

They were goddamn hot. Like hell. You moved around a lot at the plant: the rail mill rolling one day, the Bessemer furnaces the next, the pickling lines the next. For forty years. You had that mechanical ability. Cars, lawnmowers, iceboxes, bicycles. Anything.

Babe and I never worked the mill. Babe did once, for two days, and then quit. He said it was too hot: he couldn't breathe, he could barely stand up. And he wasn't even working the furnaces, he worked the soaking pits. He quit after two days and didn't tell you for a week. You knew, one of your pals at work told you, but you didn't say anything, you just watched Babe get up in the morning, walk across the highway with you, and then pretend to go to the soaking pits but peel off back home, to hang out at Gus' and wait for you at quitting time. You finally asked him for half of his weekly wage to help out with the family, and he broke down and told you. You wiped Gus' floor with him, Danny and Marty DeLuca had to pull you off. That's what I heard from Danny: both you and my brother never said nothing. Babe had two black eyes for a month.

I wasn't your favorite. I wasn't the baby, like Dorie or even Dolly, and I wasn't your helper, like Ange or Jay. You even liked Babe more, I think. I was, am, your oldest son, but I don't think you ever got over Joseph's death. The first Joe, the first oldest son. Your first boy. You even called me Joe, my middle name, most of the time. Joe or "Dreamer." "Hey Dreamer," you'd say, "c'mon and help me with the car over here." I'd come over and screw something up, and you'd send me away with a wave of your hand. I was always too impractical for you. Me and Babe, neither of us can fix anything: we can barely change a light bulb. Clumsy with our hands. Except when it comes to the girls.

58

Here old man, you want a drink of water? Or are you too drugged up? You even know I'm here? Babe's getting a sandwich, Jay and Ange are out in the hall: I think Longie's there too. Dolly's watching Dorie at home. Your sister's coming in tomorrow. All the way from New York. Jay wanted me to come in here alone. To talk to you alone. When did we ever talk?

We didn't talk, but you yelled. You yelled a lot. Pick up your room! Clean up this mess! Put the wine on the table! Even when you weren't yelling, it sounded loud. When I got drafted, and I thought they were going to send me to the Pacific, you told me to be careful, and it sounded like a shout. You yelled at Mama too. I hated that. Ordered her around like the servant she was before she married you. Her second cousin, Farrinelli, owed a favor to her father, and so allowed her the opportunity to share a room with three of her cousins and work fourteen hours a day in his grocery store and two hours a day at home. America the beautiful, eh? She was a good cook, Mama. She was twenty when she arrived, almost an old maid. You'd been here for four years already, and could speak the English pretty good. Had a good job, an American name, could fix things, not bad looking, and maybe wouldn't make her work sixteen hours a day. But there was a war on, and they didn't draft wops, and some of the lonely American girls liked your mustachio. So you waited: one year, two years, two and a half years to ask Farrinelli's servant to take that walk up Santa Fe to Our Lady of Mount Carmel. Like I said, anything's better than working sixteen hours a day.

And then the babies started coming. She was twenty-five when Ange was born. Then Joseph, who died from the flu that came home with the doughboys. Then Josephine. Were you worried that you'd be stuck with girls? That maybe you didn't have another boy bullet in your gun? Then I came along, and

FATHER

survived. Why weren't you grateful? Then Babe after me. Then Louis, stillborn, in 1926. The Congentina in '28, and Dora in '31. That was it. Mama was forty, tired. You got balance: four girls, four boys. Except the girls were stronger. Two of the boys died young, and the two who didn't were mama's boys, thinkers, dreamers who liked games and girls more than fighting and fixing things. Babe even took violin lessons. You were disappointed. You yelled. You used the belt. You yelled some more.

Then Mama died. I was twelve. You were forty-two. Still young. I remember her being sick and I remember having to be quiet when we were around the house. I remember you coming home from the hospital with your face white as a ghost. I remember Ange telling me and Babe in our room and crying crying into the pillow. I remember you yelling even more, after the funeral, as if you could scream your way through the pain. I assume it was pain, and not just anger and inconvenience.

So what do I have to say to you now? I'm sorry you're dying? Yes, I'm sorry you're dying. This is sad for me. I got no parents. But I'm going to school. Studying history, and then law. Babe too, we're both going to be lawyers. On the GI Bill. We're going to make you proud.

MOTHER

"Did you hear about Esther Tolson? She died last month."
"No, I didn't hear." "She was *my* cousin, my mother's brother's
daughter. I don't know if that makes her a second cousin to
you or not. She had cancer. A quick cancer, thankfully." I don't
remember Esther Tolson. Harry's memory is so good. He's as
sharp as a tack. "You remember Esther, don't you? She was
married to that Samuels fellow, Walter Samuels from LaMotte.
A good-looking man. Your brother knew him, was sweet on
his sister, Lottie. Charlotte Samuels. Tall and skinny, like her
brother. She died in nineteen seventy. Anyway, Walter liked the
ladies, and wasn't careful who knew about it. I don't know why
I'm telling you this; it was so long ago. Jeff must be bored silly."
"No, I'm fine." "Esther never talked much, and after Walter
started running around, she talked even less. I think Esther
came to your dad's funeral, Frances. She was a big woman, used
to wear her hair up high. Do you remember? She raised the two
children, Martha and Mabel, without any help from old Walter.
Walter died in nineteen seventy-five in a car accident. He wasn't
by himself. Esther moved to Saint Louis to be with Mabel. They
buried her here, not next to Walter in LaMotte." "Is Frances
coming? Where's Frances?" "She's right here, dear. This is her
son Jeff." "Oh. I see. Is Frances coming? Where's Frances?"

I feel so sorry for Harry. Ethel's been getting senile for a while, and Harry told me she often wakes up in the middle of the night screaming at him. Or else she wakes up and tries to get out of the house. He won't put her in a nursing home. His daughter Linda helps him, but I wonder how long he can keep her at home. "I'm right here Ethel. I'm right here." She looks at me like she is trying to remember something. "Oh, I see," she says, then looks down at her nervous hands. It's quiet for a while. I can hear the ticking of the grandfather clock in the hallway. "I didn't go to the funeral," Harry says, "because Ethel had had a couple of bad nights, and I was just too tired." Poor Ethel. I wonder how much of the conversation she understands. I look over at Harry. He's looking out the window into the distance. It must be so hard for him. Jeff clears his throat. He bends over and rests his elbows on his knees. He's not having a very good time. "I heard it was a nice funeral. I'm sorry I didn't get a chance to pay my respects."

"Hello? Dad? Hello?" "In the living room, hon. Visiting with Frances and Jeff." Linda must be home. I haven't seen her in at least ten years. "Linda does all the grocery shopping now. Most of the cooking too. I don't know what I'd do without my Linda. I'd better go see if she needs any help." Harry stands up. I need to go to the bathroom. It must have been all that ice tea. I want to meet Linda first. "Frances, you don't have to get up. I'll be right back. Would you like more tea?" "No, no thank you. I just want to stretch my legs. We were in the car all morning." "Jeff, are you okay? Can I get you another coke, or a beer." "Yeah, I'll take a beer." "You're driving you know." "Geeze Mom, just one beer." "You're from Colorado, right. You like that Coors?" "It's okay." "Well, we're close to Saint Louis. Budweiser country." "Bud'll be fine." Harry goes into the kitchen. I'm not sure what to do. I want to see Linda, but I don't want to leave Jeff in here alone with Ethel. I have to go to the bathroom. Not badly, but soon. Linda comes through the kitchen door and stands in front of me. I'm pleased that Jeff rises quickly out of his chair. Linda is smaller and older than I remember. It's been ten years, but her face has aged. She must be at least forty now. And she's not married. I married at thirty-six. I'm not sure that was such a good idea. "Frances, you look well. It's been what, ten years." "Yes, I believe so. Ten years." She turns to my son. "And Jeff. My father tells me you're teaching in Chicago. How do you like the big city?" "We like it…" "Linda!" "What is it Mother? I'm talking to Frances and her son Jeff. I'm sorry. You were saying?" "Linda! Where's Frances?" "She's right here, Mother." "Oh, I see." Linda smiles. "Some days are better than others. Do you like Chicago?" "Yeah, we love it. There's so much to do, restaurants, bars, the Art Institute, the Cubs." "It's such a big city." "Your father says you've been traveling." "Yes I have. I went to Wales last summer, and I loved it. I hiked Mount Snowden, three thousand odd feet. It was gorgeous. I'm going to try to get back this summer. Depending on how Mom is." I wonder if she went by herself. "Linda, did you get my Grape-Nuts?" Harry comes in and hands a bottle of beer to Jeff. "Thank you." Joe likes Grape-Nuts too. "I didn't see any Grape-Nuts in the groceries. They were on the list." "They went up thirty-five cents a box. It's outrageous. We're not going to pay almost three dollars for a box of cereal. There's cornflakes in there, you can finish those up." She turns to me. "I can't believe how expensive everything's getting." "No, neither can I." "Thirty-five cents more." She shakes her head. "Thirty-five cents more. And the boxes aren't that big, either."

"Goddamn it! This is the last thing I need. The very last goddamn thing. Damn damn damn. Fuck!" "Oh Jeff." "First look at the traffic, and then look at our gas gauge. I should have stopped in Joliet. If this traffic doesn't clear, we're in deep shit." I wish he wouldn't curse like that. Sometimes he's too much like his father. "I'm tired, I'm hungry, and we're going to run out of fucking gas twenty miles outside of Chicago." "Maybe there'll be a filling station coming up?" "I don't know. I just don't know. Fuck. What's the holdup? We should have taken the bus or something. I should have stopped in Joliet. I should have stopped in Joliet. I should have stopped in Joliet. No good deed goes unpunished." "Maybe there's an accident or something. You wouldn't think there'd be much traffic on Sunday night." "No you wouldn't. No you wouldn't. Dead stop. Dead fucking stop behind a big fucking truck." Please don't ruin the day. If you can't be pleasant, don't say anything. "We're going to run out of gas. We're going to run out of gas." He slams his palm on the steering wheel. "Maybe you should turn the engine off if we're stopped?" "You don't turn off your engine in the middle of the interstate at ten o'clock at night." The truck in front of us lurches forward and then stops again. "God damn it to hell." Jeff turns the radio on way too loud, then turns it down a little. It's still too loud. I'm going to think of pleasant things. It was nice to see Nadine again. I'm glad she's feeling better. I liked that funny story Harry told about my brother and the time he wore a kilt out hunting. I feel sorry for Harry and Ethel both. That's so sad. I'm glad we took them out to dinner. I haven't tasted fried chicken like that since I don't know how long. The truck in front of us starts moving, stops, then starts again. We follow, pick up speed, and soon we're in the clear. Jeff turns the radio off. "There's a filling station up on the right." "Yeah Mom, thanks, I see it." "Looks like we'll make it huh?" "Looks like we'll make it."

FATHER

"Oh God. What time is it baby? Almost two thirty? I missed Contract Law again. Fuck." This apartment is freezing. She should turn the heat up. I shouldn't have to ask her, she should know better: a guy could freeze his balls off in here. I know fuel oil's expensive, but you don't entertain a man in a goddamn icebox. No wonder I don't want leave the bed. That and her sweet little trim. It ain't cold down there.

"Where you going? You gotta go to work huh. No, she ain't expecting me until four thirty, after my class is done. I don't know. Maybe I'll just lie here and smoke: it's too cold to get out of bed. Hand me those Luckies, will you." She tosses the pack on the bed near my feet and turns to get dressed. I lean over to grab my cigs. "I just told you: if I go home now she'll know I missed my class again. All right, all right. I'll go to the library or something. Maybe go down to Jack's and have a beer. You wouldn't happen to have a fiver you could lend me, would you? What are you looking at me like that for? I'll get it back to you. I always do, don't I? I brought drinks the other night, didn't I? What? Keep your money then. Yeah, yeah, just keep it." Fucking tight bitch. Maybe it's time I dump the broad. I got enough trouble with my wife. Where are my pants? Damn it's cold. I should've never gotten involved with this miserly little cunt.

What a mistake. A lousy five bucks when I spent ten the other night on drinks at the Wyndham. "What do you mean? These are my cigarettes. Sure I'm sure." She's counting cigarettes now. Fuck this. I throw off the covers and take my pants from the chair. I start shivering immediately. One leg, then the other. Where's my shirt? I'm so cold I can hardly see straight. I curse the cow under my breath. "Fucking cunt. Fucking tight cheap whore. Fucking porca." She screams. "You heard me." Watch, ring, then undershirt, then shirt, then jacket, then shoes. I look around, find my briefcase. A present from my father. I put my overcoat on. "Fuck you, you cheap little bitch," I say right to her face. She holds her nail file in her hand like she's going to stab me. I fake like I'm going to punch her, and she throws her hands in front of her face. I turn around and back out the door. I don't want to get stabbed with that file. After the first couple of stairs, I run down what remains of the four flights to the bottom.

Marone, it's cold out here. I need a cigarette, but I left the pack, my pack, on the bitch's bed. Maybe I should go back up there, slap her around a little and retrieve my cigs. Never trust an Anglo bitch. Dark Scots-Irish. Drinks like a fish and screws like a pro. And counts like a Jew. Buttana la shaka. God damn her to hell. Maybe I should wait down here and punch her lights out. It's too goddamn cold. The bus stop's three and a half blocks. Maybe I'll warm up if I get moving.

I scratch my nose and smell that cunt on my hands. I should have taken a shower or washed up, but there was no time. I need to splash on some cologne somewhere before I go home. I don't want Enid sniffing around and asking questions. She ain't stupid and I don't need the grief. I don't know what I'm going to do until four thirty. If I had some scratch I could catch a matinee. I'd like to see that new Mitchum picture, *Night of the Hunter.* But I barely got bus fare to get home. Did I leave my tie? No, it's in my suit jacket pocket.

The cold here is different than in Colorado: it's damp and cuts to the bone. Like the people. If I was back in Pueblo, I could go to Coors Tavern, or the Star Bar in the Grove, and mooch a beer from one of the guys. Or the Veterans Tavern across from the mill. Or Tommy the Rock's place, or Jo Jo's: I could run a tab and pay them later. Here, there ain't nobody I can ask. And even if I could ask, they'd say no. Bastards. They won't even give me a fucking job in this town. After they fired me from Filene's, I've been looking for how long, six months? Six goddamn months and nothing, not even a nibble. Fucking Boston Brahmins. Anglo assholes. I'm a war veteran and I'm in BC law school, and I can't even get a job at the local Howard Johnson's.

I need dough. I can't keep asking Enid for it. My sister Dolly sends me a ten once a month, and sometimes Jay will chip in with a fiver, but other than my seventy-five from the government I got nothing else. Enid pays the rent. She's always saying something about it. Or even when she's not saying something, she's thinking about it. I'm not a fool. I tell her, "Look, I'll pay you back everything when I get my degree. You know how much lawyers can make in this town: you just got to trust me." She's just got to have faith in me. I don't know. I chip in fifty a month, which leaves me thirty. Nothing. I don't have class tomorrow, I guess I'll look at the want ads and pound the pavement. That is if Enid will pry open her purse and give me a fin for bus fare and lunch. Jesus, it's only a quarter to three. I don't know what to do for a couple of hours. I need to do something to get out of the cold. Maybe I'll go to the library. There's the bus stop. I hope I don't have to wait long.

I should have punched that whore's lights out. Marked her good. This fucking town. I can't catch a break. I get into a good law school, BC's a good school, but I can't support myself in this Anglo Irish Wasp town. Fucking Irish. Like my landlady, when I first got here three years ago, Kathleen McKinnon. She watched me like a hawk. Nosy bitch. "Where you going?" "I'm going out!" "Where you been?" "I've been working! I want no fooling around here." Took her out a couple of times, you know, to grease the wheels. She lifted up my pant leg once and asked "Where are your cowboy boots?" Thought I was a cowboy from Colorado. I should have showed her my gun. Her daughter was sweet, sweet sixteen. Sharon or Shannon or something. She liked me more than her mother did. When I got involved with Enid, the mother turned nasty, threw me out. I should have taken the daughter for a weekend, strapped her silly, and sent her back damaged goods. She would have gone with me, I know it. Fucking Irish. Jesus it's cold. Where's the goddamn bus?

MOTHER

"Corn, corn everywhere. Look at all the corn." "That's a lot of corn, Mom. So where are we going exactly? We're going to see your friend, Nadine somebody, right? And then we're going to your reunion. And then to your cousin Harry's, and his wife's, the one who's sick. And that's it, right?" "I'd like to stop into the town before we go to Nadine's, to see our old house. And then visit my folks' grave." "That's a full day." "We're almost to Barry." Jeff turns on the radio and fiddles with it for a while. Then he turns it off. I don't remember this big highway. It was built after I left. I remember Highway 36, from Hannibal to Aladdin to Hull, and then to Kinderhook and Barry. I don't like these big trucks going so fast. Jeff doesn't seem to mind them. The map says we drive on this highway until we reach exit number 20, and then turn right and go south on Rodgers Street into Barry. I used to live a couple of blocks away from Rodgers Street, on Hull and Main. I guess most places in Barry were a couple of blocks away from each other. But we always came in from the west on 36 from Aunt Helen's, and turned down McDonough by the schoolhouse. I hope I can find my way around.

"Applebasket Farms. We pick 'em, You eat 'em. Apples, Apple Butter, Apple Pies. That's cute. Did you see that sign?"

"I saw the sign." Maybe we could get some apples on the way back, or maybe a pie to bring to Lisa. I don't know if she likes apple pie or not. "Does Lisa like apple pie?" "I guess so. I don't know, Mom, I don't know." You'd think he'd know if his wife likes apple pie or not. Joe likes apple pie à la mode. I wonder how he's doing. I should call him tonight. It's nice to be away. There sure is a lot of corn. I remember detasseling and rouging some of these fields. It was hot and dusty work. I'll never forget the time I grabbed that ear full of aphids. I can still feel how awful that felt. It sends chills up my spine even now. "I think she does like apple pie." Oh.

So this is where Rodgers Road meets the highway. Look how nicely paved it is. It used to be an old dirt road we'd take when we went to the reservoir. I think it was gravel when I came back for Dad's funeral. Now it's new smooth blacktop. I don't remember Hamilton Street, but there's Union Street, where my friend Betsy Rankin used to live. I haven't thought about her in years. She used to be so pretty. All blond curls and blue eyes. I felt like a big cow next to her. Her dad died when she was fourteen and she and her three brothers and mother moved to Quincy. We wrote a couple of letters to each other, but then they moved again. I wonder what happened to Betsy Rankin. Maybe Nadine will know.

"There's Williams, there's Mortimer, stop sign, stop sign. I'm looking for Main Street." "So this is downtown Barry." "There's Main. Turn right." We pass the fire station and the old Esso filling station across the street. It looks closed. Lawrence Street. "There's Tilsons' old house. When I was a young girl, they painted it canary yellow. My dad laughed and laughed. My mother hated it." Now it's just an ugly green. I wonder who lives there now. "There used to be more trees around." "Huh." Perry Street, then a stop sign, then McDonough, where the

Koogles used to live. I never liked them that much. Their noses were all stuck in the air. "Slow down. There it is. There's my old house." "I'll park over here." Oh dear. It looks like it hasn't been painted in years. I see toy tricycles, two bikes, a green tent and one of those inflatable wading pools for children on the front lawn. There's a light blue van and broken down truck in the driveway. It looks junky. And the grass is all brown and splotchy. It could really use a good soaking. My father would never have let the house deteriorate like that. We kept our yard clean, and always had to pick up our after ourselves. We didn't have many things. Jeff parks the car and turns the motor off. It's suddenly quiet. We roll our windows down. The air is hot and humid. "It looks a little beat, doesn't it Mom? Who owns it now?" "I don't know. The Wilsons bought it when my father died, but that was almost forty years ago. My cousin Harry wrote that someone named Pritzer bought it from the Wilsons, but I can't remember how long ago that was. I'll have to ask Nadine or Harry." "Looks like they have a lot of kids. Do you want to get out? Maybe we could go inside." "I'd rather just look from here." "You sure? We could say that you used to live here. People don't mind." "No. I'm all right here, Jeff." "Do you want me to take a picture?" "I don't believe so. I'd rather remember it like it was." The car heats up quickly as we sit for a while. I remember my brother squirting me with the garden hose. I remember once when I was playing in the tree, someone must have cut it down, and Ma came out on the porch to call us for dinner. She didn't see me, and she shouted our names, then turned her head to the left and then to the right, looking into the distance. I'd never seen her before when she didn't know I was looking at her. She looked tired and old. I waited until she went back inside before I climbed out of the tree. I remember coming home from the library, the snow falling and my bag heavy, and feeling happy, because soon I would be warm and reading my new books by the stove. I wonder if I'll ever see this old house again. It's getting too hot to sit here. "If you turn right on Hull, we can see the backyard. Then make a left on the next street, Mortimer, and we can go on to the cemetery." Jeff starts the car and the air conditioner blasts on as we roll our windows up.

Park Lawn's not a big cemetery, but I've only been here two times in thirty years. I hope I can find my folks' grave. I know it's down the hill from the Jenkins crypt, but I can't remember if it's to the right or left from the main road. "Do you know where they're buried, Mom?" "They're down the hill from that big crypt, but I'm not sure if it's this way or that way." "Do you want to get out and walk? Why don't we walk around, stretch our legs." Jeff parks at the bottom of the hill under a tree and shuts the car off. I open my door, but my seatbelt doesn't slide up. "It does that sometimes. You'll have to undo it." I fumble around for the latch, but can't seem to figure it out. Jeff is stretching his legs outside. He turns around and watches me, then ducks his head back inside the car. I'm so clumsy sometimes. "Can't you get it? Here." He touches it lightly and the belt immediately retracts. I open the door wider and slowly slide my legs out. My legs are stiff and don't move easily. I manage to pull myself out of the seat and stand on the pavement. Jeff sure has a small car. I hear crickets singing. It's hot even in the shade.

"Is that it, Mom? It says 'Patterson' on it." I turn around and walk up the hill to where Jeff is. I can feel the sun on my forehead as my eyeglasses darken. I should have worn a hat. It looks like he found it. I'm surprised it's so close. I didn't remember it this far down the hill. Patterson. Frank L. 1872–1968. Margaret E. 1890–1956. I was in Elko when Ma died.

She was talking to Mrs. Poelhus, said she had a pain in her chest, and died in the house. My brother's buried in Missouri with Kay. I wonder where I'll be buried. Probably in Pueblo with Joe.

FATHER

I feel good tonight. Tommy's joint's hopping, look at all the cars. I can hear music from the edge of the parking lot. He must have a live band. Greeley's from hunger, boring. I feel good in Pueblo, Pueblo's my home. I got seven, maybe eight bucks, plenty for booze but not enough for a good time girl, unless I go to the colored girls at the Klamm Shell. I could use some strapping, but I ain't never been with a mulignan. Eggplant parmesan. Maybe Donna D'Antonio and her two friends will be here, Leftie and Rightie. She couldn't get enough of me at Central. We used to do it in the bushes near Lake Minnequa, she even wrote me a letter when I was back east. I hear she got married to Nickie De-Joy, who went to Centennial. And then to Korea. I never liked that Nickie, always a show-off son of a bitch. All the DeJoys are like that. Maybe Tommy'll lend me one of his broads, just for an hour. He's always got the dames, that Tommy, always got the dames. Single, divorced, married, tall, short, fat, skinny, blonde, brunette, mother, daughter, Mexican, white—it don't matter to Tommy—they fly around him like millers around a streetlight. I got my nice suit on, my nice tie, my Florsheims all polished: I look sharp, like a million bucks. Fairy tales will come true.

The place is packed. Tommy's moved all the tables and chairs out from the right side of the lounge and the restaurant, so people can dance near the band. I like that Mexican music, but I hope they play some older songs, some Crosby or Hoagy Carmichael. Or some Sinatra. There's Tommy, across the lounge, working the crowd. I try to catch his eye, but he's talking to a couple of tall paisans I don't recognize. I see Tracy Oreskovich and Nina Badovinic hovering around. I thought Nina was married to that switchman from Denver—Brunjak, I think his name is. I wouldn't mind getting in her caboose, that's for sure. Her brother was in the service, got killed in France. Babe knew him, played poker with him or something. What the fuck was his name? Danny? Benny? I'll ask Tommy, he knows everybody. He's busy with those paisans, so I'll get a beer and see who else is here.

The bar is packed but I squeeze in, order a Walter's draft from Tony Passerelli, and take my cigarettes out of my jacket pocket. Lucky Strikes. Maybe I'll get lucky tonight. I tap a cigarette on the bar, put it in my mouth and take out my Ronson lighter, real silver plate with my nickname, Booze, etched on it. I can feel this broad checking me out from five or six feet away. She's sitting at the bar, wearing a pearl necklace, and her brown hair is curled tight, but long, a little like Anna Magnani. Classy. It's too crowded to check out her frame, but her face is peaches and cream. I like the lipstick, not too bright. Maybe I should buy her a drink. It don't look like she's with anyone. I got the money.

"Hey Tony. Tony. What's that broad over there drinking? The one with the dark hair? And pearls? Crème de menthe, huh? On the rocks. Pour us both one." I throw a couple of bucks on the bar, like a big shot, to pay for beer and two drinks. It's almost a dollar tip. I should watch myself.

She tips her glass to me and smiles. I tip my glass to her, take a sip, set my glass down and take a drag off my cigarette.

Real cool, like Robert Mitchum. I'll go over there in a couple of minutes. I don't want to appear too eager, like some punk kid who don't know nothing. I finish my beer, then take another sip of my highball. I look at the mirror above the bar and see the reflection of the crowd behind me. Men in ties and suits, women in dresses, this is like the Ritz or some place in New York. Is that my brother-in-law, Ted? I turn around to look at him square. He sees me, but looks away, starts talking to some guy. Peter Delvecchio, his show-off friend. They're sitting at a table with a couple of dames I don't recognize. That looks like Angelo Spinuzzi. I see girls, but I don't see Mrs. Spinuzzi. I wonder if Ted's stepping out on my sister? I'll pretend I didn't see him neither. I turn back around and check the girl out of the corner of my eye. She's not talking to anyone, she's just sitting at the bar, drinking. Maybe she's a buttana. Maybe she just wants to dance.

The music stops. The band must be taking a break, so it'd be a good time to talk to her. I put my cigarettes and lighter in my pocket and get begin to move through all the people trying to get to the bar. "Excuse me, excuse me." Suddenly, I feel a tap on my shoulder. It's Charlie Tafoya, a buddy of mine from Central. His dad worked with my dad at the mill. We were in ROTC together, and he saw some action in the Pacific. I never did like his wife, Rita. Rita Fraterelli. He married her just before he shipped out. She never liked me neither. She smiles tightly and moves past me to the bar. Stuck-up bitch. "How's it going, Charlie?" "Yeah, I'm a college man. In Greeley." "I was back east, but it didn't work out." "Yeah, a thirty-five-year-old college boy." Mike was always nosy. "No, I wasn't married. Where did you hear that?" Everyone knows my business. My sisters have big mouths. I ain't going to tell nobody my business. "I'm here for a week. We could have a couple of beers, maybe at the

Veterans Tavern. Call me at Ange's. I'll see you later, Charlie." That Charlie, he's a good guy. Wants to know everything, but a good guy. Where's that dame? She's still alone at the bar.

Jesus God, there's George Vinci. I haven't seen him in ten years. He looks bad. I heard he had a hard time in Korea, got shot up or something. He never married, as far as I know. "Hey George, how you doing?" I look behind him to see if that dame's still there. "I'm going to college." "Greeley." "Yeah, on the GI Bill." "No, I haven't seen Ted. Is he here?" "Babe's doing good, he's going to law school." I can tell he wants to smoke, have a drink and reminisce, but I want to talk to that broad in long hair and pearls. I don't want to be rude to George, I haven't seen him since before the war, but I don't want that pigeon to fly the coop. "No, I didn't know that about Sam Dazzio." "They had to amputate right at the knee?" C'mon, c'mon. "No, I knew his brother. He was married to...Bonnie...Bonne...Bonnie Sabo." "She died?" "Her mother died." Jesus God this guy's depressing. Like an old woman. "And her sister's sick too. In a clinic in Denver. That's too bad." "No, I ain't married." "No, I never met your sister." "Listen, George, I need some cigarettes. I'll talk to you later." What a wet blanket. I slip past him and finally face up to the broad at the bar.

She looks good, good, better than from far away. Some dames look worse the closer you get to them, but not this one. "Hello. I'm Joe, Joe DeShell." "Jane, that's a pretty name." Like Jane Greer. "Yeah, I grew up here. I know Tommy from way back." "This is Tommy's joint." "You're from Chicago, huh?" "No, I ain't never been to Chicago." "You want a cigarette?" I hold out my pack to her. "You don't smoke, huh?" Here's Tommy now. I give him an embracito. I don't see his girls. "Hey Tommy. It's good to see you." "Yeah, I just got back today."

"This is Jane. Jane, this is Tommy." "Why, where we going?"
"You got something to tell me, huh?" "Can't it wait?" "It can't
wait, huh?" "Excuse us Jane." Tommy leads me by the arm away
from the bar to the alcove near the johns where the payphone
is. "What are you doing, Tommy, I was making time with that
girl." "Yeah I know who she is. Jane. She told me her name."
"No, she's alone. She's from Chicago." "She's not alone, huh?"
"Checkers Smaldone, huh? I heard of him." "He'd break my
legs, huh?" "Jesus Tommy, thanks for telling me. I didn't know
she was Checkers' girl." "A bunch of big shots are here for
some meeting. In Pueblo, huh? Yeah, I'll keep it under my hat."
"You gotta go. Okay, see you later." Jesus, I don't want to get
knocked around just for talking up some bird. Maybe I'll hang
around here for a while, at least until the music starts up again.
Checkers Smaldone. I heard of him.

MOTHER

I bought this yellow jacket and skirt outfit new. I hope I look nice. Jay and Ted say that I do. I think yellow is a pretty color for me. I like this jade necklace. Hmm hmm hmm. What is that song? Everybody loves somebody in the springtime? No, no. Hmm hmm hmm hmm.

Jeff is getting married today. Lisa's family is very nice, although I have a hard time remembering all of the sisters' names. I wish Joe were here, although maybe it's good that he's not. He gets so crabby sometimes, and he doesn't do so well in new places. And he'd probably want to leave early. I feel sorry for him, I really do. I'm going to try not to think about him too much. He's not here. He should be, but he's not.

The young man who's driving us is very nice, very polite. And good looking too. He told us not to worry about anything, that he'd get us there in plenty of time and that the ceremony wouldn't start without us. He's talking to Jay and Ted. My stomach hurts a little. I guess I'm nervous. I'm glad I went to the bathroom before I got in the car. I'm thankful Jay and Ted came with me. I don't know what I'd do by myself. "My doctor told me that if I needed an operation, I'd be fine, because I have no fat, no fat on me at all. It's easier to get to your insides if you don't have all that fat to cut through, like Frances, for instance. Right Ted?"

Albany is a pretty city, although I wish it wasn't so cloudy today. It doesn't feel like it's going to rain, though. At least it's not too hot.

Look at all the people. I've got my purse and I've got my camera and lots of film. That film is so expensive, but Joe said to take a lot of pictures to show him when I returned. There's one of Lisa's sisters, the blond one with the new baby. Sara? I'm not sure. The baby is cute. I've never been to a backyard wedding before. The flowers on the tables are sure pretty. Lilies and roses. There's Lisa's father, the good-looking man with the eye patch. We had a nice visit last night at the rehearsal dinner. I believe his wife is fatter than I am. Where's Jeff? There he is. He looks so handsome in his white jacket, white shirt, black pants and black bow tie. That's a lovely jacket. It's silk. He showed it to me yesterday. "Hi Mom. How are you?" "Fine, fine." "Hello Aunt Jay and Uncle Ted. Thank you very much for coming." "You're welcome, Jeff." "Here Mom, we have a corsage for you. Let me pin it on you." "It's very pretty." "You look great Mom. You remember Lisa's sister Stephanie, and her this is her husband John and their baby Reid." "Yes, I'm very glad to meet you. To see you again I mean." Stephanie, Stephanie's the one with a baby, and Sara's the one with the two small children. "I guess we're ready to start." I'm not sure where I should sit. Maybe next to Jay and Ted in the second row. "No Frances, you sit up here in the front, next to Lisa's grandfather." I see Lisa is wearing a black dress. That must be the fashion today. I don't care for it. I didn't care for their wedding invitations either. A naked man and woman looking at a sunset. I wonder whose idea that was. I guess I'm just old-fashioned.

81

There's the justice of the peace. Joe said they should get married in a church with a priest, but we had a justice of the peace too. In Santa Barbara. On our way to Hawaii. We never got to Hawaii. Santa Barbara was pretty. I wish we could have stayed there instead of going back to Pueblo. Pueblo is a nice city and all, but I like the ocean. It might have been nice to stay in California. Hmm hmm hmm hmm.

Lisa smiled at me. I'm not sure she likes me. She probably thinks I'm too much of an old fuddy-duddy or something. She's very smart, and seems a little cold or reserved. She's liberated. I hope she's not mean to Jeff. I wonder if they'll have children. Her three sisters all have children. Or is it four? I'm glad Jeff got connected with such a large family. I think it was difficult for him to be alone so much of the time. Holidays were not much fun around our house, what with Joe so crabby at Christmas. He looks so handsome up there. I wish he'd take his hands out of his pockets.

Lisa does seem like a nice girl. She's skinny and beautiful. Girls are sneaky though. She broke up with him when she was living in California. She hurt him terribly. That wasn't nice. I remember when he called and told me. He sounded so upset, like his heart was broken. I hope they have it all worked out.

I hope they have a good marriage. Better than Joe's and mine. They've known each other for a long time. I remember my brother's wedding at the church in Hannibal. It was a grand affair. Everyone was there, even Ethyl Hoyt. She had such a crush on my brother and was so angry when Kay snagged him. I still remember that cake; almost three feet high and creamy white frosting with yellow cake and chocolate crème inside. And the church was full of red and white roses. Kay's father must have spent a fortune. This is very nice too, although not as fancy. Joe will be happy that the rehearsal dinner was cheap.

"Dear friends. We gather here today in joy, to celebrate the commitment of two people to one another."

FATHER

I don't know what the fuck I'm doing. I've been married before, I've been married before, I don't want to get married again. I'm going to get trapped, trapped. She's going to tie me down that woman, she's going to tie me down. She's a nice person, she's just not for me. It's my own fault, I should never have agreed to this. I can still get out of this. I can tell her tomorrow morning that I'm not going to go through with this, this farce of a wedding. Or I could go back now, tell her tonight. It'll break her heart, but it will be better than being trapped in a loveless marriage. Or I could just leave now, go back to Pueblo, take the coward's way out. How much scratch I got? Thirty bucks of my own, plus about two hundred of her money. Can I get to Pueblo with thirty bucks? Fuck, I don't know. Goddamn women. Always trouble. Why'd this have to happen to me? Why me? I've had enough trouble with broads. I don't deserve this. I don't deserve this at all.

If I leave her now, I'll have to find some way to get her her money back. Almost a thousand dollars. Those fucking dice. I should know better than to play the dice. How am I going to tell her? I blew all your money on a crap game, so we ain't going to Hawaii? And I don't want to marry you anyway? See you in the funny papers? I ain't that big of a strunze.

"What?" "Yeah, another rye on the rocks. A glass of water too."

God my luck is bad. We kept hitting those boxcars, twelve twelve twelve, three in a row. What're the chances of that? I was down five hundred in five minutes. And then I tried to make it up. That was stupid. I should have listened to my brother, he don't never play craps or roulette, only blackjack and poker. I can hear him now, "You gotta watch out for the table games, Frank, the odds are heavy with the house." He's a smart man, my brother, a smart man. I never liked that bitch he married, that big-mouth from Oklahoma. She's a redhead too, like Frances. A loud-mouth, redhead, red-faced Oklahoma bitch, first class. Vulgar, that's the word I want to use, vulgar. She don't like me neither.

"Thank you." The whiskey tastes okay. Where's my water?

What the fuck am I going to do?

Frances wants kids. I want kids too. Boys, boys to carry my name into the next century. Three of my sisters got kids, but none with our name. That Oklahoma bitch is barren. Babe told me her first one, the son she had with that cowboy husband in Texas, messed her up inside so she can't have any more. That was stupid marrying her. Babe loves kids, and he married a loud-mouth Anglo-Saxon bitch who'll never give him anything but grief. All the nice Italian girls he could have had, all the young girls from Pueblo who could have given him babies, and he chose that used-goods barren whore from Oklahoma. She's been around the block two or three times, that bitch, don't tell me she hasn't. Two or three times at least. I don't understand that marriage. I shouldn't make the same mistake. I should wait, marry someone twenty years old, someone dark and Italian who loves the strapping and having

85

babies. Someone from the old country, with dark hair and dark eyes and who don't speak English. Someone who'll moan and whimper when I'm giving it to her but'll thank me later. That's what I want, not some spinster schoolteacher from Illinois. How the fuck did I get myself into this?

I should have learned from Enid, from the disaster of my marriage with Enid. Another Anglo, a Boston Anglo. God, they can't leave us alone these nervous Anglo bitches. I should stay away from Anglos, all Anglos. I should stay away from women. They're all liars, every last one of them. I should just fuck 'em and leave 'em, that's what I should do, fuck 'em and leave 'em. I didn't want to marry Enid, and I don't want to marry Frances. I was trapped by Enid, and now I'm trapped by Frances. I repeat myself: she's a nice woman, she's just not for me. She's not my type. I should live alone. I'm a loner, I like being a loner, I like what I am. I don't want to be trapped into living with a woman I don't love.

What are you looking at? Mind your own goddamn business, four eyes. I give him the evil eye and he looks back down at his beer. Maybe he's a fairy or something. This place is a dump. Everyone's getting ready for tomorrow night, except for these lushes. Who stays out until one thirty on New Year's Eve morning? I should go back to the hotel. What am I gonna tell Frances?

This whisky burns, and that bastard, he forgot my water. I already tipped him two bits. No one cares about their job anymore. This ain't the Ritz, but you'd think the bartender'd bring you a glass of water when you ask for one. I could understand if he was busy, but there are only four other mokes here, and they're all half asleep. This joint ain't exactly hopping. No one takes pride in their work, pride. Look at me, I look nice. One thirty in the morning and I still got my suit and tie on. And my hat, right here on the bar. J.P. Dillard, Boston Massachusetts, paid thirty bucks in 1950. Probably cost me fifty today. I'll wear it tomorrow for the wedding. Get a shoeshine too.

I don't know, I don't know. If I decide to ditch her, what do I do about the grand? And if we do tie the knot, there's nothing that says I can't get a little on the side. I'm a young man, and men have these, these needs. We'll live in Pueblo, and there're a few buttanas I can make in Pueblo. We'll have some kids, two or three boys, to carry my name on. Babe can't have any kids, unless he gets rid of that red-haired whore. I gotta do it, I gotta do it. "Last call huh?" "How much I owe you?" "Three dollars, huh? You forgot my water." "With my last drink you forgot my water."

We got the rings already, we got the rings.

MOTHER

I like it when Jeff is home. I know he doesn't like to come home for Christmas. Who would with his father acting the way he does? He's usually quiet and doesn't talk much when he's here, but it's still nice to have him around. I don't have many people to talk to, and Joe is so crabby this time of year. I know that both of his parents died in December, but that's no excuse for being so mean all of the time.

I like this song. This used to be Jeff's favorite carol. "Do you remember how this used to be your favorite carol? You used to sing 'pa rump pa pum pum, rump pa pum pum, rump pa pa pum.'" "Yeah, I remember." "If you turn it up too loud, your dad will come up." "Screw him. It's Christmas Eve." "You shouldn't say things like that." "I know, Mom, but he's such a jerk. I don't know how you put up with him. Or why." I don't know how I put up with him either. He's gotten so bad in the last few years, so crabby and bitter. I don't think it's his fault, I think there's something wrong with him, something wrong in his head. I wish he'd go back to that doctor. He used to be so funny. I used to laugh and laugh at the things he'd say. And now he's so, he's so I don't know what.

"You want some more eggnog Mom?" "No, I don't believe so. Are you hungry? There's some salami there, and

Zoelsman's bread, if you want to make a sandwich. There're apples, dates, some fruitcake, some patica from Auntie Jay, Italian cookies. There's cheese and crackers, potato chips and dip, nuts, Christmas candy, pizelles…carrots, celery, oranges…" "I can get something if I want it. This eggnog's kinda sweet." "Turn it down. TURN IT FUCKING DOWN!" "Your dad's yelling. We'd better turn the TV down." "We can barely hear it now. Jesus Christ it's Christmas Eve. Fuck him." "Oh Jeff. Please don't put me in the middle." "Okay, okay. There. I can barely hear it. No way he can." "So when should we open our presents?" "Tomorrow I guess. Unless you want to open them now?" "No, I can wait until tomorrow. When did you and your mom and dad open presents?" "Christmas morning. We'd have to wait until Aunt Helen and Uncle Ray came over, and my brother and I would be just silly," I hear Joe stomping up the stairs, "running around the house and shrieking like little devils. We'd drive your grandmother crazy." Oh no.

I can barely recognize him as he appears at the kitchen door. His face is twisted by hate and sleep. His light blue robe is tattered, and his big toe is coming through his left slipper. I went to Kmart and bought him a new pair of slippers for Christmas. "Deck the halls with boughs of holly," sings in the background. "What are you looking at?" he growls, and it sounds like a bear almost. "Turn that goddamn television off. I need my sleep. Turn it off now! And don't wrap no present for me, I don't want nothing. I lost my mother at Christmas. I hate fucking Christmas." "Falalalala lala la la." "What are you looking at?" "Nothing," Jeff says, and his face looks a little like Joe's. "I ain't looking at nothing." Joe cuts across the living room and turns off the TV, then stomps heavily to the bathroom and slams the door.

"Asshole." I wish Jeff wouldn't curse like that. "Just try to ignore him. He'll go back downstairs pretty soon, and we can have some chips and dip." "I don't want chips and dip: I want Christmas music." He gets up off the chair and turns the TV back on. Silent Night. "Oh no Jeff, don't. Please." I hear Joe yelling from the bathroom. "Please Jeff, turn it off. For me." "No. Fuck him. He's not going to do anything. Let's have some dip now." I hear more yelling from the bathroom, then Joe throws open the bathroom door and stomps screaming into the living room, "I told you to turn that off. I don't care if it's Christmas, I lost my mother at Christmas. Turn that crap off. I said TURN THAT CRAP OFF!" Who is this wild man? What have I done? His robe is halfway open, his white hair is matted and his eyes are almost shut with hate. "Turn that TV off Frances, before I break it. And then I'll break you." Jeff stands up and faces Joe. He's about a head taller than his father, but thinner. Please, don't fight, not on Christmas Eve, please. Please God. I think I can remember the words. "Silent night, holy night, Son of God, love's pure light." Jeff starts singing with me. Joe moves toward the television, but Jeff steps in front of him. "Please don't fight. Please. It's Christmas Eve. Jesus, Lord, at Thy birth; Jesus, Lord, at Thy birth." Joe brushes past Jeff and walks over to the Christmas tree. He looks at me, then grabs it near the middle and smashes it to the floor.

I hear glass break over the music.

Still looking at me, he walks into the kitchen. I can hear his heavy footsteps on the stairs.

I don't know what I've done. I stayed with him for Jeff's sake, but that wasn't right. And then I couldn't leave, because that would mean I was wrong all that time and wasted all those years. And he loved me once. And he was funny once. And wives are supposed to stay with their husbands, especially when things don't go well. You're not supposed to just leave.

And I didn't want to waste all of those years. I didn't want to waste all of those years.

"Are you okay Mom?" Jeff's kneeling down and picking up some of the glass. I'd like to tell him some of this. Explain things to him. But I can't. It wouldn't be right. It wouldn't be fair. "He really did a job on the tree." "Yes, I'm fine. Oh dear. I'll go get the broom. Be careful with that glass." "I'll get the broom. You sit there for a while. Do you like this song? Do you hear what I hear, do you hear what I hear?" "Yes, I do like this song. Maybe we could have some chips and dip now?"

When we get the tree up again, it doesn't look half bad.

FATHER

Today's the day, today's the day. I'm going to be a father. I pray to God it's a boy, I pray to God it's a boy. I want to pass on my genes, my legacy, my name. Joe DeShell and son. George DeShell. I'll change my name back to Fruscella like Babe did. George Fruscella. I'd like you to meet my son the lawyer, George Fruscella. Frances doesn't like that name George: she wants to call him Harry or Patrick, after her brother. Or Jeff. I like George. I hope it's a boy.

Girls are no damn good. Look what women have done to me. That bitch Enid, throwing me out of her house, calling me a two-bit hustler. What a mistake it was to marry her. And that whore, Kathleen McKinnon. Where's your cowboy boots? I should have fucked her daughter good. Got her pregnant and left town. I never should have gone to Boston, that no-good Anglo city. I want a son. A son I can be proud of. Frances wants a son too. Okay God, we both want a boy. Maybe You can give me a break this time, huh God? Maybe You can give me a break.

I gotta get something going. God damn it, I should have stayed in law school. I could be making good money by now. Me and Babe, have our own practice. We should both have stayed at Denver University, we'd both be lawyers by now. Frances has got a good job, teaching's good work, but I've got to get something. Get a good job and move out of this bastard's house. He ain't doing me any favor, renting that house for a hundred a month. I'm going to tell him one of these days, I'm going to tell him. Once I get a good job and we get our own house, I'll tell him to his face, I'll call him a bastard, right to his face. I ain't afraid of nobody. Cheap son of a bitch. Cheap son of a bitch. He's a friend of Jay's, he ain't no friend of mine.

There's not much bread left. Frances didn't do the grocery shopping last week. The nurses said it would probably be a couple of hours, so I came home for a sandwich. I could have stayed at the hospital and got something at the cafeteria, but I don't like waiting around, waiting around. Waiting around, that kills me. I want to save my money for cigars. Some El Productos. A box of El Productos. Cigars for my boy. Zoelsman's bread, Genoa salami, some butter, better than anything at the hospital. Man, I'm tired. It's almost seven o'clock now, and I took Frances in at ten last night. I could use a little shut-eye, a little nap. Maybe I should clean up, shave, look nice. I need some coffee.

I'm not sure I'm ready for this. Frances wanted a child, Frances wanted a child. I didn't want a child. I have things I want to do, I don't want to be tied down. I need to establish my career, get things going. I got some action on the side, sure I do, what man doesn't. Frances was pregnant for nine months, and for these last five she didn't want to be touched. I'm young and healthy, a good-looking guy, and I'm not going to go without strapping for five or six months. Even in the army, I'd get some every other week. I was careful, and I didn't mind paying for it. Babe liked to gamble, I screwed around. Nothing wrong with that. I didn't hurt nobody. Enid didn't care. I think she was screwing around too, that's why she threw me out. Frances wouldn't like it, Frances wouldn't like it at all. But I can keep a secret. I don't tell nobody. Like the man said, variety's the spice of life. And I like spice.

I didn't even want to get married. It was too soon, too soon. I left Enid four years ago. I needed more time, more time. But Frances was thirty-six, she was desperate to land me. I never should have gotten married so soon. She's a good woman, but I'm not sure she's right for me. I need to be alone and now I've got a kid coming. God this is not how I planned things. I get sidetracked, sidetracked all the time. I should have known better: stay away from the women, stay away from the women. Women are my downfall. But I blame myself. I know I should stay away, but I can't. And now I'm going to be a father. With a woman I'm not sure I love. Oh God.

I should have thought of this before we got married. I should have thought of this before I got her pregnant. I don't want to be tied down to a family right now. I want to try to go back to law school, or get my career going some other way. And now I got to worry about a kid. How am I going to get something going when I got a kid, a wife and kid tying me down? How am I going to do it, how am I going to do it? God damn it, how am I going to do it? I should have never gotten married. This kid is really going to fuck me up. That's right, he's going to fuck me up, he's going to fuck me up good. Look at all this crap around here already: a crib, a tub, clothes, toys, diapers…where we going to keep all this stuff? We live in a small house, a small house, and we got all this crap, filling it up. I got no room to move, I got no room to move here with all this crap, surrounding me, surrounding me up to the ceiling. God damn it Frances, what have you done to me? What have you done to me? This baby's going to fuck me up good.

There's the phone. It's probably one of my sisters wondering why I'm not at the hospital. "Hello? This is Mr. DeShell. She did huh? Already? A boy?! A boy?! You're sure? I'll be right there. Everything is okay, huh? With my son? And my wife? Yes, yes. Thank you doctor. The nurses told me it would be a couple of hours, that's why I came home. It was fast, huh doctor? Yeah, fast. Okay, thank you doctor. Anything else to tell me? I'll be right there. Okay bye."

MOTHER

Jeff's coming home from college for Thanksgiving on Wednesday, so I'll try to get some extra things to eat. And the turkey. I hope I can find one that's not too expensive. I'll make that Stove Top Stuffing. I'm sure I'll have to spend more than the eighty dollars, and Joe will have a fit, but he'll just have to have his fit. It's Thanksgiving after all. Joe gets so crabby all of the time, especially around the holidays. I really miss Jeff. I'm glad he's coming home.

There sure are a lot of people at King Soopers today. I always start on the bakery and bread side and move my way over to the frozen food, through the meats and finally to the fruits and vegetables. It might be a good idea to go over and try to get a turkey first, before all the smaller ones are taken. I don't want to end up with a thirty-pound turkey. But I think I'll just follow my routine. I don't want to get mixed up. It's already going to take me an hour and a half.

I like King Soopers. I like it much better than Safeway or County Market. County Market has cheaper prices, but you have to bag your own food. I just don't like touching my groceries that many times. Plus it's not as clean as King Soopers. It's hard to have to learn a new grocery store. I like knowing where things are. I only went to County Market once, and it took over two hours. I'd rather shop at County Market than Ralph's though. It was embarrassing having to shop for groceries on credit. Ralph's store was tiny. He hardly had *anything*. And his prices were out of this world they were so high. Joe liked his sausage and French bread. He did have good sausage but the bread was from Zoelsman's. I can get Zoelsman's bread at Safeway. I think King Soopers' French bread is just as good. It was hard to find enough variety. Joe would complain about how we'd have the same things all of the time, and I'd say of course we have the same things all the time, Ralph has nothing else to buy. I shopped there for over fifteen years. I'm sure glad I don't shop there anymore.

Joe likes the doughnuts that are on sale. I'll get a couple extra of the chocolate frosted for Jeff. He used to like chocolate frosted doughnuts, I imagine he still does. I'm not quite sure what he likes now. He doesn't come home much. I can't blame him. Joe is so difficult and they fight all of the time. I'll buy a couple of loaves of their French bread in case Jeff wants sandwiches. I'll get a loaf of Wonder for Joe too. Joe really likes bread.

I'd better check my list to see what kind of frozen food we need. We like these pizzas, these Totino's Pizzas. I remember one time Jeff had his friends over after school, and they ate all three of these pizzas I had in the freezer. And then they went out for band rehearsal or some other thing, and I had to clean up that big mess right when I got home from school. I wasn't angry that he ate the pizzas, but that he didn't clean up. He didn't have friends over to the house that much though. His dad was always so grumpy, always yelling at him or at me. I don't know why he has to be so hateful. I hope I remembered my pizza coupon. Here it is: three for the price of two. I hope I have room in my freezer for the pizzas and the turkey.

I'll get canned peas and corn, they're cheaper than frozen. Look at all the people here. There'll probably be a real mob tomorrow, after the Broncos play. I hope they play well tomorrow. My kids all wore orange yesterday, all except Arthur Vigil, who just moved here from New Mexico, and Jennie Duran, whose mother isn't married and I don't think takes good care of her. I feel sorry for Jennie. I know she gets a free hot lunch and I wonder if that's her only good meal of the day. That reminds me, I need to take down my Thanksgiving bulletin board from the main hall on Monday. I used my old Thanksgiving bulletin board again this year, where I made a list of all the words we get from the Indians and then cut out pictures from magazines to go with the words: igloo, chipmunk, kayak, moccasin. I've used that same one for I don't know how many years. Mrs. Channing, the new second grade teacher, does beautiful bulletin boards. She had one with puppies and kittens and goldfish, it was really cute. She has a baby and a cute little three-year-old and I don't know where she finds the time. She says she has a husband who helps around the house. I wonder what that's like. I need spaghetti for tomorrow. Spaghetti every Sunday. I have some frozen meatballs and sauce from Jay.

Look at the crowd around the turkeys. I'll get one of those cooking bags to roast it in. It keeps the turkey moist and won't spatter my oven. Let's see what they have here. Fifteen pounds, we'll be eating leftovers for a month. Fifteen, sixteen, eighteen, twelve, this twelve-pounder seems nice, but it's a Butterball, and they're more expensive. "Excuse me. I'm sorry." That lady almost dropped a turkey on my hand. That lady is wearing gloves. That's smart. Fifteen, fifteen, twenty, twenty-five, ten! Even with Jeff here, ten pounds should be enough for a meal and a couple of days of sandwiches. Joe doesn't like turkey that much and neither do I.

I need cranberry sauce, those cooking bags, and I'll get some candy. Jeff used to like that candy corn, so I'll get a bag of that. And potato chips. And maybe even some dip. This is going to be an expensive shop, and I haven't even looked at the meat yet. I have to get some pop too. Maybe a six pack of Coke and six-pack of 7Up. I'd love to get a couple of shrimp cocktails, but they're probably too expensive. Maybe some frozen breaded shrimp wouldn't be too bad.

FATHER

Joe DeShell, a.k.a. Frank Fruscella, a.k.a. George Melanchory, is fifty years old today. Fifty years old. Half a century. I'm going to spend a little money for a change, have a couple of drinks, live a little. I got that fifty Jay and Ted gave me, plus that twenty from Chuck. Tommy always has money. Maybe we'll have some champagne. I got the world on a string hmm hmm hmm.

My fiftieth birthday. I don't look fifty. I'm driving Jewell's Firebird with her to meet Tommy the Rock at Mr. Z's, a nightclub in the Springs. Tommy the Rock will be sure to have some broads with him. Too bad Domenic is sick. I told Frances that I was going down to the Knights of Columbus, but I don't think she believed me. Screw her. She doesn't know fun. If she hadn't gotten so fat, maybe I'd be with her more often. She can watch the fireworks at home with Jeff. The two of them deserve each other. My wedding ring is in my pocket.

Jewell looks good. I like when she puts her hair up like that, it looks real classy. Silk stockings, none of this panty hose like Frances wears, silk stockings with garters, a beautiful dress, nice high heels, real style all the way. No wonder a man wants to be seen with a broad like her on his birthday. Any man. She's got some nice legs too, and a nice rump. I don't like them too skinny. Shapely. A buttana in bed, but real class on the street. Real class.

I don't feel guilty. Screw that. Frances let herself go, especially after having Jeff. I should probably leave her, them, find myself a nice Italian wife, someone from the old country, a wench who cooks and cleans and keeps herself up, and who straps like a buttana. Tie her hair to the bedpost and make her yell, like I did to that Italian girl in the Queens, Anna Di Prima. Her brothers didn't appreciate that, so I left town, heh heh. Someone who straps like an animal, but classy when we go out. Someone I'm not ashamed of. Like Jewell. A man's got a right to do all the strapping he can. Even at fifty.

I deserve a good time, God damn it. What's gone right for me lately? Nothing. A man needs a little success in his life, a little fun. Life's been rough, rough. But I've stood up to it. Alone. I haven't hid behind any organizations. I stand for what I believe in. I like what I am. I like what I am. I deserve this.

The engine is too big for this car; it doesn't ride smooth. Not like my Olds. It was a good idea to go to the Springs. "Why do you want the trouble, Frank, let's just go to the Springs, nobody knows you there"—Tommy the Rock's idea. And Domenic was all for it. "I know some girls, Tommy knows some girls, I'll leave Genevieve at home, it'll be fun Frank, a real blast, just like old times." But Domenic's sick, so it's just me, Tommy and Jewell. Plus whoever Tommy can scare up. There's his car in the parking lot, a maroon Eldorado. That's a good car. I should get me one of those.

This is a nice joint: mirrors, red carpet, dark wood. Ten bucks just to get in. I'm already down twenty. This is going to cost some dough. There he is, in a booth, surrounded by two nice-looking girls, a blond and a brunette. Goddamn Tommy the Rock can always get the dames. Even when we were in high school, they'd be hanging off him. He'd be working at his mother's joint on Route, cooking and serving and cleaning up, and they'd be all over him, waiting until he got off work, three or four going in and getting food at closing time, and eating it slow, slow until he had to kick 'em out and make 'em wait outside. He was like a quarterback. Better than a quarterback. I didn't do too bad myself, but not like Tommy. "Hey Tommy, how ya doing? You remember Jewell. Yeah, yeah, Mr. Patriot, born on the 4th of July. Hello Margaret, huh, excuse me, Marguerite, and Louisa, hello Louisa. How ya doing? Call me Frank. Call me Frank, call me Frank. Not Joe, Frank. Thanks. You know Tommy, we always dressed up in our day: even to school, a suit and tie, every day, a suit and a tie. And the women, the girls I mean, wore dresses, dresses, none of this pantssuit crap. Every day in high school a suit and a tie. Or at least a sport coat. Except for Thursdays. Thursdays we wore our ROTC uniforms. You didn't go for ROTC, did you Tommy? No, you had to work, that's right. You still wore a tie and jacket, didn't you? Not like these hoosiers today. Long hair, dirty jeans, basketball sneakers, slacks on women.... What? I always wear a hat. Yeah, I'll have...what are you drinking, Tommy? I'll just have a beer right now, a Budweiser. And a what? A whisky sour for the lady here. Yeah, thank you. They have cigars here? You have cigars here? Give me an El Producto. Thank you. What? How old do I look? No, I'm forty-five. That's right, forty-five." Someone kicks me under the table. I don't give a damn, I'll tell them what I want: they're just a couple of Tommy's good time girls, what do I care how old they think I am?

"Tommy and I go way back, way back. We were stationed together in the war, but we knew each other before that, in high school, Central High School in Pueblo. Before that even."

"You went to Strack, right? Strack Junior High and Mount Carmel Catholic Church." "Thirty, thirty-five years I've known this guy." "Thank you. Oh, you don't have any El Productos in the glass tubes, do you?" "No?" "Thank you anyway." "We have a tab, huh? I like my cigars in tubes. This isn't fresh. They need to be in tubes, tubes." All this money for a lousy cigar. I can't get a break. "You got a camera, huh Tommy. Do I want my picture taken? I don't know if I want my picture taken. It might fall into the wrong hands, ha ha. Sure." I like having my picture taken. I remember the first time I ever had my picture taken was when I was a senior in high school. My parents never owned a camera. Make sure my tie's straight. Slide a little closer to Margaret. One arm around Jewell, the other on Margaret. She likes it. Okay. I've got the world on a string… "Cheese."

MOTHER

"Hey Frank, just in time for the chow, huh?" "I've been busy, Longie, I've been busy." I turn my head to see my husband. He looks good, in his maroon sport coat, gray slacks, white shirt and blue striped tie. He's wearing sunglasses and his straw hat, and he's smiling. I don't know whether to trust that smile. I don't know where that smile has been. I stand up to get in line for the buffet.

"Frances, get me a plate." "No, I will not get you a plate." I'm tired of this old joke. He does this every time. He wants people to think that he can order me around like a servant. He thinks it's funny. And he's so loud. "C'mon Frances. Get me a plate." "No, I am not getting you a plate." "Where's Jeff?" "He was playing pool I think." "Babe and Virginia coming?" "I don't know. I haven't seen them. Where've you been?" His face darkens. "I've been around, that's where I've been." "Hi Frank. What are you drinking?" "A beer, Ted, a beer. You got Walter's?" Ted laughs. "Walter's? This ain't Gus' Tavern, Frank. Walter's. I got cans of Coors and bottles of Lowenbrau." "Coors is fine. Coors." "You can't find Walter's any more, Frank. I heard they're going to close the plant." "They're going to close the plant, huh? That's too bad. I like Walter's beer. Walter's is a real Pueblo institution." "Pueblo's dying, Frank. Pueblo's dying."

I move inside and get in the buffet line. I can smell the spaghetti sauce and roasted peppers. I'm hungry. There's Jeff, talking to one of the Mastro girls. He has a beer can in his hand. I don't know where he got that. Dr. Mastro's girls are so lovely, so high class. I've almost finished my gimlet. It was good but I don't believe I'll have another. Ange is helping Jay serve the food. She's never been that friendly to me. She's not mean, like Dorie, but she makes me think that I'm not good enough for Joe. I'm good enough for Joe, all right. Is Joe good enough for me? If his sisters only knew half of what he does.

Look at all the food. There's a big bowl of homemade spaghetti, a big bowl of homemade cavatelli—Jeff calls them little bullets—and a big pan of stuffed shells, all surrounding a large tureen of sauce. I see platters of meatballs, stuffed peppers, Italian sausage, chicken in sauce and that rolled steak, I'm not sure what it's called, brasciole I think. There are casserole dishes of green beans, fried eggplant and roasted potatoes, with smaller bowls of roasted peppers, lupini beans, pickled artichokes and black olives scattered around. "Hello Frances. Where's Jeff?" "He was right here." "Help yourself, Frances. There's salad, garlic bread, Parmesan cheese and salt and pepper on the table. Do you want a plate for Frank?" "Thank you Ange. He can get his own." I love Jay's spaghetti and meatballs, but I want to save room for everything. I take a little spaghetti, a meatball, a stuffed shell, half a piece of brasciole, and a small slice of eggplant on my plate. I rearrange things and clear a corner, where I put a half-tablespoon of green beans. I take the ladle and apply some sauce to my spaghetti. "You should put some gravy on the meat, Frances. And the green beans too. That's the way we do it." I let a little dribble on the sausage and brasciole. I don't know what to do with my empty drink cup, so I bring it with me outside to one of the tables on the lawn.

My glasses take a while to darken, and the bright light makes me squint.

I'm sitting next to Stubby Dell. His wife, Eileen, is across the table. Longie is next to me on the other side and his son, Bobby, is next to Eileen. Jeff is sitting at another table with the Mastros, and Joe is down at the far corner with Mrs. Piserchio and Mr. and Mrs. Patti. Joe doesn't even make the effort to sit with me. The Pattis' son is sick with cancer. Stubby's hard of hearing, so everyone has to shout at him. He and Eileen are almost seventy. I've scrunched my napkin down into my collar so it protects my front. It probably doesn't look very nice but I don't want to get spaghetti sauce on my dress. I realize I'm sitting between Stubby and Longie. How funny. I'll have to tell Jeff.

I'm full. I didn't finish all of my brasciole. I don't know why I took all that food. Everything sure was good. The salad was delicious. Jay makes the best Italian dressing. Stubby's mopping up the sauce on his plate with a piece of garlic bread. Joe does that as well. If we ever did that at my house, my mother would rap us on the knuckles with her wooden spoon. I'm getting a little heartburn from that spicy sausage. Ted poured me a glass of wine. I don't care for wine, but I don't want it to go to waste. I wish I had some 7Up. I'm sleepy from all that heavy food. I have to go to the bathroom but I can wait. "You should drink your wine there, Frances, it will help you digest." Longie points at my wineglass with his fork. He has spaghetti sauce high on his cheek, almost near his eye. I take a sip from my glass. I don't think it will help my digestion.

People are getting up from their seats, stretching and walking around. I think I'll get up and go talk to Jeff. I don't want the wine to go to waste, so I take another drink. I've finished almost half. I get up and walk over to Jeff's table. He's talking to one of the Mastro girls. He looks up at me as I approach, but keeps on talking. I see he's holding an empty wine glass, and there are two beer cans near his plate. He shouldn't be drinking like this. "How much have you had to drink?" He looks up at me, smiles meanly, and then turns back toward the girl. "Frances, why don't you sit down?" It's Dr. Mastro's wife. I don't remember her name. "You don't need this anymore, do you?" I sit, and she gently removes the crumpled napkin I'd stuffed in the front of my dress. It looks pretty spotted. I'd forgotten all about it. "No, no, I guess not." I must have looked a sight.

I sit there for a while, watching Jeff talk to one of the Mastro daughters. No one else says anything for a while. Finally, Mrs. Mastro says, "Eddie's gone to get some cake. I'm sure he'll want to say hello. You remember my daughters, don't you Frances? This is Terry, and that's Jenny over there talking to your son. Terry's a senior, and Jenny's a sophomore at East." "Hello." "Hello." "Hello. You have a son too, don't you?" "Yes. Eddie Jr. He's visiting his cousin in Michigan." Jeff stands and excuses himself from the table.

FATHER

He was driving too fast, too fast. He was a good boy, a good-looking kid, and polite, but they were driving too fast. Showing off for a girl. Damn kids. Ted and Jay shouldn't have bought him that car, that sports car. Fiberglass. Who makes a car out of fiberglass? He was in high school, what did he need a sports car like that for? Oh God. Oh Jesus God.

And the mooks I got to face tomorrow. How'm I going to face those sons of bitches, those sneak thieves and drug addicts? I'd trade ten of them for Bo. Twenty. The whole fucking lot of 'em. He was a good boy, that Bo, a real nice kid. And tomorrow I gotta deal with those scum down at juvie. I don't know why I stole that car, I didn't take her purse, It wasn't my dope. I don't know how I'm going to take it.

My sister's something else. Look at all this food: roasted peppers, cavatilles, her meatballs and sauce, salad, all done up nice. Ange and Dorie helped, but Jay did most of it. Maybe she's keeping busy so she won't have to think. I haven't seen her cry. Ted's a mess, face all puffy, but I haven't seen my sister cry once. She looks a little white, like she's wearing a mask. She should cry, scream, slam a door, something. Maybe she does in private. I don't know.

Who's that? Who's that screaming? Oh, that's Ginny

Delvecchio. I never liked her. She wouldn't give me or Babe the time of day in high school. And now she's over here with her sunglasses and her hair all messed, wailing like it was her son who got killed. Who drove a fiberglass car eighty miles an hour into a light pole. She's all show, she's all show, and she's causing a scene. She ain't helping anything. Why doesn't her husband do something, give her a drink, or slap her or something? I always wondered who wore the pants in that family. Big shot Peter Delvecchio and his stronza wife. That's terrible, terrible the way she's carrying on. Finally, Ange and Dolly pry her off Jay and lead her into the next room. They ought to take her outside and hose her down, the show-off bitch.

Jesus God, what a life. Our family never had any luck, no luck at all. Bo was our best, and now he's gone. Christ. There's Frances and Jeff, sitting there by the fireplace. Bo always loved Jeff, would always have time for him, take him to the movies, play catch, everything. Even when he went to the academy in Canon City, every time he'd come to Pueblo he'd stop by. How many kids in high school do that? Jeff will never be as good as Bo. I shouldn't think that, but it's the truth. My boy's got no confidence. He's a mama's boy, a mama's boy. Christ.

I should get a plate. I'm not hungry, but I need something to do. There's my brother, making a sandwich. I wonder where his wife is. I hate that woman. She's always in my business, always in my business. She watches me like a hawk, that bitch. I don't know why my brother married her. She was married before, damaged goods. He should have married someone to have children, not that loud damaged goods buttana from Oklahoma.

I'll get myself some sausage and bread and make a sandwich. "Poor Bo." "Yeah, it was a nice service, very nice, very nice." "No, I didn't hear that." He was trying to join a club, the hundred-mile club, where they drive a hundred miles an hour through Pueblo on the freeway. "From 13th Street to the Lake Avenue exit, huh? A hundred miles an hour." Goddamn kids. "Maybe that other kid was driving, huh Babe? That Dickerson kid?" "No chance huh?" "Oh, you talked to the police. I didn't know that, you talked to the police." "Yeah, it's a sad day, a sad day." "I don't like closed caskets either, but I guess he was pretty beat up. Poor Bo. I like that picture they had on top, that picture from the Abbey. That was a nice picture." "He was a good-looking kid, a good-looking boy." "No, I haven't seen Patti. I saw her at the funeral, but I haven't seen her here." "She's taking it hard, huh? That's what you heard." "There she is, over there by Bobby and Marilyn. She looks okay from here." I take a bite of my sandwich. It's good. I must be hungrier than I thought. "This isn't Ralph's is it?" "This sausage, Jay didn't get it at Ralph's did she?" "Oh, this is from Johnny's on Abriendo. Johnny brought over a couple of pounds, and some cold cuts for today. It's good: it just doesn't taste like Ralph's." I see Babe's wife out of the corner of my eye. I don't want to talk to the nosy loud bitch. "I'll talk to you later, Babe." I put the rest of my sandwich in my mouth, grab a napkin, and move quickly away from the table. Maybe I'll go outside to finish chewing. I have more sandwich left than I thought.

I need a beer or some wine to wash this down with, but I don't want to go back where damaged goods is hanging around, waiting to say something bitchy. I walk over to Jeff and Frances. "Jeff, Jeff, go get me a beer from the fridge." "You heard me. Go get me a beer. A Walter's beer. Go on. Walter's." He gives me a dirty look, that dreamer. At least he's good for something, the mama's boy.

I stop in front of the plate glass sliding doors. There's that loudmouth, Ginny Delvecchio, talking to Stubby right in front of me on the patio. I finish chewing and wipe my hands and face on the napkin. I feel some sausage grease, maybe I should clean up in the can. I need to get away from all these people, all these social parasites and show-offs who like funerals and a free meal. Social parasites and show-offs. This should be for family only. Family only. I wipe my hands again and stuff the dirty napkin into an empty glass on the bar.

I turn and walk across the room, up the three stairs to the bathroom. The door's closed, and I hear water running. Goddamn it. I walk further into the hallway.

This was his room. Look how clean and neat it is. It's immaculate. Look how he made his bed. Tight, that's how Jay taught him. Always make your bed and always keep your room clean. Spotless. Like he was in the army.

I remember this little white stuffed dog. I don't know when he got it. I think he wanted a real dog, but Ted doesn't like dogs. And Jay doesn't either. We had a dog, Patches. He choked on a chicken bone. Oh God, why did Bo have to die? He was just a young man. Oh Jesus God. Oh God, why? God damn you, God, God damn you.

"I'm just sitting here Jay, just sitting here." "You're always going to keep his room like this, huh? Just like he left it." "What am I going to do, Jay, what am I going to do?" "No, I have to face those kids tomorrow, those dummies down at juvie, and I gotta try and straighten 'em out, and I'm going to keep thinking about Bo, and his picture from the Abbey, oh Jesus God, Jay, Jesus God. How am I going to look at those kids? How am I going to look at those kids?" "No, I have a handkerchief here." "I don't know what to do." "You're right." "I know Jay, I know." "He's with God now, huh? You believe that, you believe that." "He's with God, huh?" "I don't know." "I'll be all right, Jay, I'll be all right."

MOTHER

I like coming to these dinners. Everything's so colorful, the food is so good, and I enjoy visiting with the old Box Elder ladies. Sometimes I wish Joe would come with us and not drive separately, but it's probably better this way. He can leave early if he wants to. Everyone knows how crabby he gets. Jeff and I will have a good time.

I do wish I had one or two nicer summer dresses. I've had this old peach and lavender thing for I don't know how long. I hope I didn't wear it to this party last year. No, it was cool last year and I thought it might rain, so I think I wore my yellow skirt and jacket with a white blouse. Maybe no one will notice me much.

Oh, look how all the tables are arranged in the backyard, with the red and white tablecloths against the green lawn. I don't know how Jay does it. She makes all the spaghetti by hand, makes meatballs, cooks the sauce, fixes all the salad and the dessert, and then lays out a beautiful table. I have a hard time getting dinner ready for Jeff, Joe, and myself. And her house is always immaculate too. Even after Bo died, she still does things so beautifully. There's Ted, he's always so nice to me. He looks so stylish in his gray V-neck shirt, his white pants and white shoes. His face looks a little tired today. Jay told me he hadn't been feeling well. "Hello Frances, glad you could come. Jeff. What can I get you to drink? Some of the ladies are drinking gimlets." "I've forgotten what a gimlet is." "They have vodka and frozen limeade." "Oh dear. I guess I'll try one. Not too strong though." "Jeff?" "I'll have a gimlet too?" "Frances?" "He doesn't need a gimlet." "Mom!" "Okay, he can have a small one. But just one." Jeff doesn't need a drink. He's only fifteen. He doesn't need to start drinking at fifteen.

I wonder if Babe and Virginia are coming. It's sad that they have moved to Walsenburg. It's just not fair, the way they treated him, firing him and all. Jeff and I should try to visit them more. I know Babe's not feeling well. I hope they come today.

I'd like to try to help, but I know Jay doesn't like anyone else in her kitchen. I'd just get in the way. I walk over to the shaded porch, where Ted hands me a clear plastic cup with my cold drink. It takes a while for the lenses in my glasses to lighten in the shade. My drink tastes tart and a little like the medicine I used to have to take sometimes when I was a child. I haven't had vodka in for I don't know how long. Maybe ten years. "Hi Frances. Where's Joe?" "He'll be along soon. He has a meeting this afternoon." I don't know why I said that. His sister Dorie knows I'm lying. She's a lot like Joe. Mean. That's why she asked me that question. She's wearing an expensive-looking black dress, high heels and black stockings. Lots of jewelry. "A meeting on Sunday?" She's not a nice person. She looks young for her age though. "Hello Frances, how are you? You remember my mother, Louisa? Mom, this is Frances DeShell. Joe's wife." "Who?" "Joe DeShell's wife. Frances. She doesn't remember so good anymore. Jay Ciavonne, this is her house, her brother is Joe DeShell, this is his wife, Frances." "I don't know no Joe DeShell." I take another sip of my cold drink as Mr. Spinuzzi leads his mother inside.

113

There's Mrs. Piserchio, sitting on the lounge chair. She used to babysit Jeff ten years ago. She must be almost eighty by now. I'll have to get Jeff to come say hi to her. "Hello Mrs. Piserchio. I'm Mrs. DeShell. Do you remember you used to babysit my son Jeff?" "Of course I remember. Frances, right?" She was always sharp. "Yes." "Sit down, Frances. Is your boy here?" "Yes he is. Somewhere." I look around, but can't find him in the yard. "Maybe he's playing pool in the rec room." I sit in a wooden chair. It feels good to sit. "How's he doing, your boy? He was smart as all get-out, and sweet too. He was shy. Is he still shy?" "Yes, I suppose he is." "How old is he?" "Fifteen." "Does he have a girlfriend?" "No, I don't believe so." "Shy. Bashful. That's okay, you know? I always liked your boy. Is Frank here?" "I don't believe so. Not yet." She nods, then leans forward and picks up her purse, opens it, and rummages around. The skin on her face is brown, the color of the stain on Ted and Jay's house, and finely wrinkled. She's wearing thick, black framed sunglasses, like Joe's. She holds out a piece of wrapped candy. "Butterscotch?" "No, thank you. I have this drink." I like butterscotch, but I don't know how it would taste with my gimlet. "I smoked cigarettes for fifty years, Frances. Winstons at first, then Pall Malls, then Virginia Slims. My doctor said if I didn't quit smoking, I'd die. So I quit. And now I suck on these butterscotch candies. I can go through a whole sack in a day. Did you ever smoke, Frances?" "Yes I did, when I was in college. Everyone smoked back then." "When did you quit?" "When I had Jeff. I didn't really like it much, so it was easy." I can see my reflection in the dark lenses of her glasses.

I look down and to my right, to a small table with wooden bowls of nuts and yellow lupini beans and a stack of red and white napkins. I take one of the oily lupini beans and squeeze it out of its skin with my thumb and finger into my mouth. I like the texture and the salt. I take another one, then wipe my fingertips on a napkin. I don't see anyplace to put the skins, so I wrap them in the napkin I've just used. I'll hold on to it until I find the garbage. The tartness of my gimlet goes well with the salty oil of the beans. I'd like to take another but maybe I'll wait. My stomach growls. I hope Mrs. Piserchio didn't hear it.

"Hiya Frances." There's Longie. He's the husband of Joe's oldest sister, Ange. He's always so polite, and tells funny stories. He has an artificial leg from the war that gives him trouble. "Hello Longie, how are you feeling?" "Oh, can't complain Frances, can't complain." He sits heavily in a chair beside me, his artificial leg stiff and unbending. "And if I could, who would listen?" "Longie. What can I get you to drink?" "Hiya Ted. I'll just have a can of beer. Coors if you got it." "Coors it is. Frances, how is your gimlet?" "It's very good." "We'll be sitting down soon, but help yourself to the lupinis and nuts." "Oh I will, I will." "Where's Frank, Frances?" "He came in a different car. Said he had a meeting this afternoon. I don't know if he's even here yet." "He's a free spirit, that Frank. A free spirit, eh Frances?" "He's a free spirit all right."

"Okay people, let's eat. C'mon. Bobby, Angelo, Peter, go on, get in line. First in line gets a prize." "What's the prize, Ted?" "You don't have to wash dishes. That's your prize."

115

FATHER

"Goddamn kids! Get off my fucking grass!" Day after day they have to play on my lawn. "I should have never moved here Frances, I should have never moved here." I can't get any rest. "I never should have married you, Frances, never should have married you. I don't care; I don't care who can hear me. Let 'em hear, these fucking neighbors, what do I care?" I never should have married her, look how fat she is. "Look how fat you are. You must weigh three hundred pounds. I'm going to leave you, Frances. Leave you and that weak son of yours." Where is Jeff? Is he playing next door? Two against one, all the time. Two against one. I'll put the hose on those kids, that'll stop them. I have a right to water my own yard. Look at what they're doing to the grass. "Play in your own yard. I know that's your yard, but this is my yard. This is my property. I have a right to water my own yard. Play in your own goddamn yard." Smart-aleck kids. Goddamn punks. No respect. "Listen you smart-ass kids, from the driveway to here is my property, and I don't want you ruining my lawn. Go to the park to play." "I'm crazy? I'm a crazy man?!! What are you, you smart-ass punks? Where are your parents? Go home. Leave me alone. Leave me the fuck alone. And stay off of my grass!" That negro boy, what is his name? I never liked him. I never liked any of them.

Especially their fucking parents. The cowboy next door with his dogs, barking barking every time I go outside. I could strap his daughters, though. Especially the older one. Buttanas. Hippies. I got to get off this block. Where's Jeff? "Frances, where's Jeff? JEFF. JEFF. Where is he? Frances, answer me. ANSWER ME! Where's that son of yours?" When my father called, we came quick, or else we got smacked. A weak kid, that Jeff. A dreamer. Always moping around. The moper, that's what I call him, the moper. "Frances, where's the moper? What's he doing downstairs? I need him to drag hoses. Jeff. JEFF. Come up here, I need you to drag hoses. I've been working since six o'clock. I can't do all this work by myself." I'm tired, I'm tired. Goddamn this door. Open up you son of a bitch, open up. I need to fix this fucking door. You'd think Jeff would fix it, the lazy kid. Always moping around, reading. Or listening to that goddamn music. He's got no ambition, no initiative. He looks like a goddamn question mark. The question mark I call him. "Move that hose over there, by the ash pit. Not there. There. THERE. Stand up straight. Move this one and the one in the front in fifteen minutes. Whatya mean, you won't move the one in front? Your friends, your friends. They're just a bunch of punk kids, your friends. They called me a crazy man. Get out of here, then. Go back inside and help your mother. Mama's boy. The question mark. The moper." Fucking punks, still at it with their football. "Ah shut up you fucking dog. SHUT UP." Everything's against me, even the dogs. Trapped in a loveless marriage with a spineless child, a dead-end job, can't sell real estate in Pueblo, everybody's leaving Pueblo, no money, maybe I can borrow some from Chuck at Texaco, he can put it on my credit card. I should have stayed in law school. I should have stayed back east. Married some nice Italian girl, had a bunch of children, children with respect. I'm going downstairs, where it's

117

cool, to rest. Look at this mess. Unfinished basement, concrete walls, naked light bulbs, laundry on the lines, it's like a prison down here. I'm in exile. But it's cool and I'm tired. I got up at five this morning. I can't sleep at night. I'll lie down for a while. God I'm tired. God, what's He done for me? No wonder I don't go to church. I believe in the holy catholic and apostolic church. No more. No more. I don't know why they gave up the Latin. And now they have mokes with guitars at Mt. Carmel. And the way people dress. When I was young, we wore a suit and a tie, a suit and a tie to mass. We didn't wear sport clothes, tracksuits and sneakers. A suit and a tie, our hair combed. We looked nice. Not like these mokes today. Even when they do wear skirts, these bitches, they only do it to show their legs off. Asking for a strapping. I'll oblige them, the buttanas. I should go down to the lounge tonight, help Carlo out. Jewell Turpin won't be there, still seeing that Anglo landscaper from Fountain. Always showing off with that motorcycle of his. I haven't fucked her in two, three years, and I still help out at the bar. For what? A lousy fifty a night? Carlo gets at least a hundred and fifty on Saturdays and Sundays. At least. She sure played me for a sucker, that horny bitch. Calling Frances up after I fell behind on a payment, that fucking whore. I should have slapped her around a little bit, taught her a lesson. Then she called my sister up. All because I was a week late. I still owe her what, a couple thousand? They're all alike, these women, all buttanas. I hope Jeff can stay away from all these horny bitches; they'll ruin him like they ruined me. Buttanas have been my downfall. Buttanas and the Anglo-Saxon racist town of Pueblo Colorado. I'd like to make my case to the United Nations, about how this racist town, the Thatchers, the Sam Jones and the *Pueblo Chieftain*, all conspired to kill my brother. You talk about conditions in South Africa, you need to talk about conditions right here in

Pueblo Colorado. I can hear those fucking kids playing again. How can I get any rest? Day and night, day and night they play play play. "PLAY YOU FUCKING PUNKS, PLAY!" God damn it. If only one thing would have worked out for me, one thing. No. Not my career, my marriage, my son, my civil rights work, not one goddamn thing has ever worked out for me. I have to live in the middle of a goddamn playground. I should have never married Frances. I should have never come back to Pueblo.

How I hate my life. God how I hate my life.

FATHER

MOTHER

I'm glad fifth period is over. Fractions are always hard for the kids to understand at first. And little Marty Ruiz, I thought I was going to have to send him to Mr. Potestio's office, he was being so naughty. His parents are nice people, I think he's a dentist and she works as a receptionist in his office, but their son sure is wild. Maybe he'll grow out of it. Jeff didn't always behave himself either. He used to tell stories. I remember when I had a parent teacher conference with Mrs. Ramirez, she said how wonderful it was that Jeff and I had traveled to so many places. We did go to Barry a couple of times, once to see my family and once for my dad's funeral, but he told his class that we had visited New York, Hawaii, Los Angeles and even France. I didn't say anything, but I think Mrs. Ramirez knew we didn't really go to all those places. I was embarrassed, but I'd rather he tell stories than turn out mean and hateful like his dad. I don't know if I'm doing such a good job with Jeff.

I like fourth period this year, when the kids do their reading. I'll try to mark a few penmanship exercises while they're busy with their SRAs. Or maybe I'll review my lesson plans. I'm glad we don't do the speed reading unit until next month. I can never get the machine to work and all that back and forth makes me dizzy. The SRAs let the children read at their own speed. I think that's better, and so does Mrs. Anderson. Jeff was always so good at the SRAs. I believe he finished them all one year. He loves to read. I'd like to get a drink of water but the bell's about to ring.

"Boys and girls, boys and girls. Today we're going to read our SRAs. Please take out your workbooks and pencils. Clint, Clint! I'm surprised at you! Please leave Estrella alone and sit down at your desk." "But I need to get my exercise, Mrs. DeShell." "You sit there, and I'll bring your exercise to you. The rest of you may get your exercises now. What color and number do you need, Clint?" "Copper. Copper seven, no eight. Copper eight." "Mrs. DeShell, Mrs. DeShell." "What is it Melinda?" "Juan took my exercise." "It's not yours. I'm working on it too." "Did you try the other box, Melinda?" "No." "Try the other box and see if you can find it. If not, skip that exercise and work on the next one."

I'm tired. I was on my feet since first period. The kids wore me out. They had to stay inside for morning recess and lunch, but they were so mischievous we decided to let them play outside in the cold in the afternoon. I hope no one's sick tomorrow. I already had three out today.

I'm cooking hamburgers tonight for dinner. I hope I took the meat out of the freezer this morning. I'm not sure I did. If I forgot, we can get McDonald's or something. Joe will complain, but he'll complain anyway. He never cooks. I don't think he can even boil water. I have ten dollars in my purse, that should be enough for McDonald's. I like their fish sandwiches. And there won't be as many dishes.

It gets dark so early these days. At least it's not snowing. I'm glad I don't have to drive to Beulah or Rye, I heard they got eight inches last night. The roads are clear. Joe's car's not in front of the house. Good. It's funny how I used to feel bad when he wasn't home, and now I feel bad when he is. Sometimes when I see his old car or hear him coming in the back gate, my heart just sinks. That's not the way it's supposed to be, I know. He used to be so funny. Now he's just crabby all of the time. I hope he stays away for a while so I can sit down, relax and read the paper.

"Jeff? Jeff?" Nobody's home except for the dog and me. Jeff might still be at band practice. "Come here, Star, come here little doggie. Do you need to go out?" He's not going to want to stay out too long in the cold. "That's a good boy, that's a good doggie. Come on inside now. Good boy. I wonder if Jeff gave you fresh water this morning. Did he? I'll give you some right now. Your bowl's almost dry." I give him a couple of dog biscuits. I see I did take the hamburger out of the freezer after all.

I need to get out of my girdle. I'd better turn out the light: I don't want to give Mr. Johnson a free show. That feels much better. I need a new housedress, this one's falling apart. There's Mr. Tate across the street, smoking on his porch. He must be freezing. Mrs. Tate won't let him smoke inside. She's a nice woman. She brought over a couple of zucchini and some tomatoes from her garden last summer, and we had the nicest visit. Or was that the summer before last? There's Mr. Elizondo coming home. I haven't seen Terry around much lately. I heard she had her baby. Look at all the cars across the street. There's five in the driveway and four out front. Three families live in that one house, but they must be having some other people over. There are always a lot of high school kids over there. Joe calls them hillbillies, and says he's going to call the police on them. He thinks they're selling drugs. The Ruigs still have their house for sale. She got a job in Colorado Springs, and they moved six weeks ago, but they still haven't sold their house. Joe says they want too much money. Mrs. Ruig always had such nice clothes. They didn't have children, and they both had good jobs, and so why not buy some nice things? I could use some new dresses. Some of my school clothes are over ten years old. Next door looks like she went grocery shopping.

It's getting chilly in here. I should turn on the heat. Not much mail. Just the gas bill. And the Sears' bill. Let's see here. It feels good to sit down. Joe always messes the paper up, I can hardly find the front page. Look at all those poor people in Africa. I don't even know where Cotonou is. Oh dear. I feel so sorry for those people. They want to close the Pueblo Army Depot. Dorie works there. I wonder what the weather's going to be like. I hear a car door slam. It's almost time for the news on channel eleven. I wonder if it's Jeff or Joe. If it's Joe, I'd better start dinner. I stop reading and turn my neck to look out the living room window, but the drapes are closed. I sit quietly and listen.

Father

"MERBISC—Most Extraordinary Recreation Bargain in Southern Colorado. We've got tennis courts, an Olympic size pool, a spa, a clubhouse, and a golf course—eighteen holes. All brand new. We've got two restaurants right now, with more coming in. All twenty miles south of Pueblo on the way to Walsenburg. We'll take a drive there, Mr. Gonzalez. Is there a Mrs. Gonzalez? The three of us will take a drive out there, you can swim, play golf, do anything you want for free, and then I'll buy you dinner. Would you be interested in that, Mr. Gonzalez? Can I make an appointment with you? No, you're not ready yet, huh Mr. Gonzalez? I must tell you, I got some nice parcels, you really need to see them. And they're going fast. I got in on the ground floor myself, Mr. Gonzalez. Can I make an appointment with you? You're just not ready yet, huh Mr. Gonzalez? It would just be a couple hours of your time. No? Mr. Gonzalez, if you change your mind, please give me a call: Joe DeShell at 542-5173. That's Joe DeShell at 542-5173. Thank you Mr. Gonzalez."

These leads are crap. I've been calling for two hours and nothing. Phone book leads, I call them. Phone book leads. It's been what, fourteen months since I closed a deal? Over a year. And Giadone still gave me a big ham five months ago for Christmas. He went to school with my brother. Now he's carrying me. Colorado City's good property, glad I got two lots myself, right on Ponderosa Drive, near the lake. I gotta make a sale to keep up the payments or I'm going to lose them. Frances won't pony up, she's so goddamn shortsighted, says we need the money for Jeff's school. Jeff's school, Jeff's school, why can't he get a scholarship or something? I've got one of these properties in Jeff's name. He can sell it in four or five years if he needs tuition. He's such a mama's boy anyway. Not practical. This real estate, it's for the family, not for myself. She should trust me. "Hello, is this Mr. Douglas? Mr. Douglas, I've got one word for you: MERBISC."

How long does it take to play a goddamn round of golf? They've been out there for two hours, while I sit at this bar, drinking my coke and trying to look busy. I should have brought a newspaper or something, but that might not look professional.

My sisters love golf. I never played. Stupid game. Walking out there in the hot sun, hitting a little ball with sticks. Jay and Ted are out there every Sunday. Screw that. Ange is a good golfer. And Dolly and Dorie too. Only me and Babe never played. It costs money and it's a waste of time. Like this trip. If that Higdon and Jack are brothers, I'm the pope. They're just jerking me around, wasting my whole afternoon so they can mooch a free round of golf. Higdon didn't look that interested when we drove by the parcels, didn't even want to get out of the car to see those cheaper lots on Beaver Creek. And he was looking out the window when I showed him the models of what they think this will look like once it's developed. They couldn't wait to get out there on that golf course. What a sucker I am.

I'd like to get a beer, but I don't know how much longer those freeloaders are going to stay out there. I have to drive them back, and I want to have a beer with them with they come in. Show them I'm a regular guy and all. Psychology. I'll buy them each a Budweiser. I have a ten and some ones in my wallet. They give us credit here. Maybe we'll have a couple of beers. I have to drive them back, so I'll just have another coke now.

Maybe I'll walk around a little, get some air. I did say I'd be here at the bar when they came back, so I guess I'll stay put. Not that it's going to do me any good. He ain't going to buy. He's probably not even a fireman. I should have never gotten into this racket. After Bo died, I couldn't keep working at juvie, with all those mokes and minchiones, but I should have found something else to do, something where I didn't have to talk to people all the time. They're just askers, all of them, askers and takers. Never give me a goddamn thing. Nobody's any good. And real estate in Pueblo, what a joke. Everyone's getting the fuck out, like rats off a sinking ship. Soon as these kids graduate from high school, they go to the Springs, or Denver, or Boulder, or somewhere far away, fast as they can. Pueblo's dying. Pretty soon, it will be all old people. A goddamn ghost town. I should get the fuck out too. I need a fresh start. Maybe California or someplace.

Here they come now, clomp clomp clomp on those ugly shoes. "Hello Mr. Higdon, how's it going? Lemme buy you a beer. Three Budweisers please. Do you have the long neck bottle? No? That's okay. How did you like the course, Mr. Higdon? Oh, a little windy. More challenging then, huh Mr. Higdon? Thank you." I like Budweiser in the tall bottle, not cans. Nothing goes right for me. I'll use a glass. "Mr. Higdon, did you give any thought to the parcels I showed you today? Did you talk it over with your brother? Would you like to be near the lake, or do you think the Beaver Creek area would suit you? You didn't discuss it much, huh? Kept your mind on your game. That's good, that's good. I should have been out there with you today, huh? No, I don't play golf. My sisters all play, but I can't seem to find the time: always trying to make that deal, you know? Do you want to drive by any of the lots on our way home? After we finish our beers. I bet golf makes you thirsty, huh Mr. Higdon? You need some time to think about it. Okay. Do you want to talk to your brother now? By yourselves? I can take a walk. No, you need some time. Okay. I understand. Don't want to take too much time, though, the lot you want might be gone. I've seen it happen. Sometimes you gotta strike while you can. I wouldn't want you to lose something you really want because you hesitated. So you want to drive by after we finish our beers?"

MOTHER

"Frances! Frances! Get up, Frances. It's six-thirty. Get up Frances, get up Frances. Let's get going. C'mon."

Oh dear. It's six-thirty already. It seems like I only went to sleep an hour ago. Joe's pacing kept waking me up. He paces all night sometimes. He's so nervous, he makes me nervous. I'm sleepy.

"Frances! You forgot to make my orange juice. I need orange juice in the morning, Frances, I need orange juice. You know I need orange juice Frances, you know I need orange juice. C'mon. Get up."

You'd think he could make his own orange juice. It's not that difficult. I'm tired. I have playground duty during lunch period all this week, so I can't go over my lesson plans until this afternoon. I might have to drink two cups of coffee this morning.

"C'mon Frances, hurry up. Use the bathroom Frances, so I can get in there. You got to make my orange juice, Frances. I want waffles this morning. C'mon, let's get going. It's snowing outside. You'll have to leave a little early. Frances!"

All right, I'm getting up. I do need to use the bathroom. And then I'll make his orange juice. And fix his breakfast. I hope it's not snowing hard. The kids go stir-crazy if they can't go outside for recess or lunch period. They can get so naughty. I look out the window. It's wet, fluffy snow. The roads don't look too bad. I hope Joe has at least turned the coffeepot on.

"Frances!"

"I need waffles, Frances, waffles." "I'm making your orange juice. I can only do one thing at a time." "Hurry up." "All you have to do is put them in the toaster." "You do it. That's why I got married." "Do you want Aunt Jemima or Karo? "Both." "You don't need both." "I want both." I get the two bottles of syrup out of the refrigerator and set them on the table. The Aunt Jemima's almost gone. I'll have to put it on the grocery list. I take two waffles out of the freezer and put them in the toaster. I take the hamburger out to let it thaw. After Joe's waffles pop up, I'll have toast with my coffee. Toast and strawberry jam. Here's Jeff. "Morning Mom." "Good morning." "Dad." I try to be cheerful for Jeff. "Would you like some breakfast? I can make you some eggs, toast, bacon, waffles, cereal…" "No, no thank you…" "French toast, sausage, fruit, did I say cereal? Oatmeal…" "Why don't you ask me if I want those things?" "I know what you want." "No, nothing Mom, thanks. I'm not hungry. I'll just have some juice." Jeff doesn't eat breakfast anymore. "I remember when you used to eat cereal every morning. We used to have five or six boxes in that cabinet below the radio, and you used to pick and choose from Apple Jacks, Frosted Flakes, Quisp, Cap'n Crunch, Lucky Charms, Cocoa Puffs, Honeycomb, Alpha-Bits. Sometimes you'd even have two bowls. I thought I was giving you a good breakfast, and I find out later they were all nothing but sugar." "I don't know, I'm just not hungry for breakfast. My stomach's not ready." "It's the most important meal of the day, breakfast. The most important meal of the day." "How about some toast, or an English muffin with jam? There's good Italian bread to toast." "I'm not hungry, okay. I'll just have juice. Jesus, leave me alone." Jeff's crabby this morning. The whole house is crabby. He drinks his juice in one gulp and sets the glass down hard on the table. "What's the matter with you?" Joe asks with his mouth full of waffle. "Was' da muttuh wf ewe?" "Don't you mock me, you little bastard." "Don ewe mock me, ewe lil batherd." "Get out of here then, get out of here you son of a bitch." "I'm leaving." Jeff stomps out and Joe turns to me. "I blame you Frances, I blame you. You've spoiled your son rotten Frances, spoiled him rotten." I take another bite of toast and sip my black coffee. This jam is good. I swallow my blood pressure pills with another sip of coffee. They're so big, like horse pills. "I blame you, Frances, I blame you." What else is new? He blames me for everything. "Mom? Mom? Have you seen my blue and white striped shirt? The one Aunt Virginia gave me?" "Did you look in your closet?" "Yes I looked in my closet. And it's not there." "It must be downstairs then. I don't remember ironing it." "Could you iron it for me this morning? Mom?" I suppose I could give it a quick once-over. If I do it now. I don't want to be late for school. "I suppose." I finish my coffee and stand up, put the cup and my little toast plate in the sink. The breakfast dishes will have to wait. I hope Joe won't make a fuss. "Never mind, I found it." "Where was it?" No answer. It must have been in his closet all along. "Where was it?" I ask louder. Still no answer.

"Hello Mrs. DeShell." "Hello Anita. How are you?" "Fine Mrs. DeShell." Poor little girl. I don't think she has a very nice home life. Her mother's on welfare, and I don't think the father lives at home. She's got three or four brothers and sisters, and one of the boys is always in trouble. But the girls are as sweet as can be. Anita's shy, but she's very smart, she reads and reads and reads, and her penmanship is beautiful. I think they all get a free school lunch. Her mother's nice enough, she comes to all the conferences, but I think she's more interested in finding a husband than in making her kids do their homework. "It's cold today, isn't it Anita?" "Yes, Mrs. DeShell, it's cold." "Is your coat warm enough?" It looks like a good coat, although she doesn't have a hat or mittens. "Yes, Mrs. DeShell." "Do you have a hat? Or mittens?" "Yes Mrs. DeShell. See? I took them off in the bus and put them in my pocket."

I like Lakeview. It's cheerful, even in winter. I like the way the hallways smell like the heat from the furnace in the winter, the office smells like coffee in the morning and mimeograph fluid in the afternoon, and my homeroom smells like paste and crayons. I don't like the way the cafeteria smells, like sour milk and tomato sauce, and the old bathrooms smell like old bathrooms, but my homeroom is far enough away that I don't notice. There's Mr. Taravella, the coach. "Hello Frances. How's that boy of yours?" "Hello Coach Taravella. He's fine, he's fine." "He still at Roncalli?" "No, he goes to South now." "He a freshman?" "No, a sophomore." Mr. Taravella whistles. "Time flies, Frances, time flies. He still skinny? And smart?" I smile. "Yes, I suppose he is." "The kids will be inside today, so I got to go set up the gym. See you later, Frances." "Goodbye Coach." I need to run off a spelling test. I'd better do it now. Lunch period can be so hectic, and I have playground duty.

FATHER

"Look at this room. Look at this room. God, how can you live like this? You live like a pig." "I came from a motherless home, a motherless home, and I picked up after myself. We all did. We never lived like this." "That's right, that's right. We all picked up after ourselves. Our house was neat as a pin. Without a mother, our house was neat as a pin." "You take after your mother. Not after me, after your mother, your mother's side of the family. The Anglo side." "How do you live like this? You're a pig." "I won't stay out. This is my house, my house. I can go anywhere I want, anywhere I want." "Shut your mouth. I do too pay for it. I do too pay for it, goddamn it." "I have a job, I sell real estate. I have a job, you little pig, you little bastard. I sell land. Where do you think I go everyday?" "I'm a salesman." "And I fight for civil rights. I'm not part of the Anglo system like you. That's what I do, that's what I do all day. I fight the system." "What do you know? You don't know nothing." "Look at you. Stand up straight. You look like a question mark." "You live in this filthy room like a pig, and you can't stand up straight. And that hair, God that hair, you look like a wild animal." "That's right, that's right, like a wild animal. Are you human?" "Tell me Jeff, are you human?" "Don't tell me to shut up, you little bastard. Don't you ever tell me to shut up.

You show me some respect, you little bastard, you show me some respect." "I have earned respect, Jeff, I have earned respect." "You have your mother fooled, but not me. You don't have me fooled. I see you, I see you." "I see a wild animal who can't stand up straight. Who lives like a pig. No wonder the girls don't go with you. Who'd want to go with a pig like you?" "When I was your age I dressed nice. Nice shirt, nice shoes, a haircut, a tie. Not like a goddamn animal at the zoo. You're not human." "You go fuck yourself, you little bastard." "What a thing, telling his father to go fuck himself. What a thing, what a thing. A thing an animal would say." "God you disgust me." "I never liked you, Jeff, never liked you. You disappoint me, you disappoint me deeply." "What have I done for you? I gave you life, that's what I've done for you. What have you done for me?" "I had to get married because of you, and look at you. God." "That's right, I had to marry your mother because of you. I never wanted to get married and I never wanted you. You forced me into this marriage." "This loveless marriage." "That's right, that's right, I never wanted you." "You disappoint me. You disappoint me deeply." "You're not a go-getter, Jeff, you're not a go-getter. When I was your age I was working, helping my family out. I didn't stay at home, moping around the house, my face buried in a book. No, I worked. And went with girls." "I don't see you going with girls." "Don't you try to shut the door in my face, I'll knock the hell out of you. I'll go to jail, I don't care, but I'll knock your teeth out if you do that again." "I don't care, let the neighbors hear. Fuck the neighbors. That's right, fuck the neighbors." "You're the animal. You're the animal." "I'm ashamed of you, Jeff, I'm ashamed of you." "Turn that off." "I don't want to hear that jungle music, turn it off." "I said turn that fucking thing off or I'll turn it off." "Oh yeah? Yeah?" "I'll turn it off for good." "You think I won't, you little bastard?" "There." "I told you to turn it off. I told you I didn't want to hear it." "I don't care. I don't care, you little bastard." "I told you to turn it off." "It's your fault. It's not my fault, it's your fault." "I told you to turn it off." "I don't care. I'm sick of that jungle music." "Look at you, how hateful you look. How hateful." "Tell your mother. That's right, go tell your mother. Mama's boy. Mama's boy." "Get out of my sight."

Everyone's against me, everyone's against me, even my son. Goddamn mama's boy. He's a major disappointment to me, a major disappointment. He's got a lip on him, I'd like to punch him in the mouth. Slap him around, like my father did to me. I never would have said those things to my father: he would have taken me out in the backyard and beat the hell out of me. Telling me to go fuck myself. My father would have beat the hell out of me. I blame his mother for turning him against me. Two against one all the time, two against one. And the way he looks. With that posture and that long hair. The question mark. He's a stranger to me. Oh God.

I pulled the wires out pretty good. He likes his music, his jungle music. Takes after my brother. My brother used to play the violin, until the kids teased him, so he quit. I like music too. The songs of the forties and fifties. "Embrace me, my sweet embraceable you." I remember my father bringing that old Philco home when I was a kid. Someone had given it to him because it didn't work. He fixed it up in no time, and we listened to Amos 'n Andy and Jack Armstrong, *Jack Armstrong, The All-American Boy.* He could fix anything, my father. He could fix this hi-fi in a snap. I just broke the wires, I didn't pull them out. I'll get my electrical tape and join the speaker wires again. I'll strip the wires, twist 'em together and tape it all up, it'll be good as new. I ain't going to buy the mook a new hi-fi.

"What does it look like I'm doing?" "Hand me that roll of tape there, will you? Over there. There. By your foot there. There." "Take the scissors and cut this tape." "I wrap each wire, and then I wrap the whole thing together, see?" "It shouldn't come loose for a while, but be careful moving the speakers."

"Let me get out of the way, and you can test it out." "Turn it on." "Put the record on, see if it works." "Not too loud, not too loud."

Little punk doesn't even thank me.

MOTHER

Joe's already left. He doesn't like fireworks because they remind him of the war. That's what he said. Babe was in the war and he loves fireworks. Joe just doesn't like children. Or maybe he has somewhere else to go. I don't mind. He can go you-know-where for all I care.

Babe sure likes kids. Virginia too. I wonder why they never had any of their own. I know it's none of my business, but it doesn't hurt to wonder. They were in their mid-thirties when they got married, but so were Joe and I. Joe blames Virginia, but I don't know if that's true or not. Joe and Virginia don't get along. She says, "I was raised in Oklahoma and in Oklahoma we don't take any crap off men." Too bad I wasn't raised in Oklahoma.

Jeff loves fireworks. He hasn't been able to sit still since we arrived. Bo and Bobby like fireworks as well. I don't think Marilyn and Patti appreciate them much though. "You like some more wine, Frances?" "I believe so." "Give me your glass, hon." She takes my glass and fills it to the top. Oh dear. I meant to say I didn't want any more. "Another hamburger? Hot dog? Babe's got some fresh ones, hot off the grill." I've only had one hamburger, and if I'm going to drink some of this wine I should have more to eat. I don't know. Jay thinks

I'm overweight. I guess I am. "We got more than enough, Frances. He's got a mountain of meat on that grill." "I'll have another hamburger, yes, please." "Longie? Robert? More wine? Beer? Another hamburger or hot dog?" "I'll take another hot dog. And I'll get myself another beer." "Longie?" "Nothing for me, thanks Virginia." "There's a cooler down here, Robert. You don't have to go all the way to the kitchen." "Thank you Virginia, but he's got Coors upstairs." "We've got Coors down here, too," Virginia says under her breath, "he just wants to go up and hit Babe's whisky. I don't mind the drinking, it's the sneaking around." "I think Dorie minds the drinking," Longie says. "And there're kids around." "When you're right, you're right, Longie. Where's Joe off to, Frances?" "I don't know, Virginia, I don't know." She shakes her head and gives me a sympathetic look. She says just loud enough for Longie and me to hear, "This family, this family…"

"It's almost dark, Aunt Virginia, it's almost dark. When can we start the fireworks? Can we light some bottle rockets now?" "We'll have to wait until your uncle finishes cooking." "He says he's finished now and to ask you." "People are still eating, honey. Do you want a hot dog or hamburger?" "They can watch and eat at the same time." "Jeff," I say, "don't be rude." "Maybe we should start. Babe went overboard as usual: he must have a truckload of fireworks in the garage. Okay, honey, you tell your uncle to start setting up."

I've never cared for fireworks. I always think they're going to shoot off into someone's eye. I read in the paper where some kid in Pueblo lost four fingers of his right hand. Babe is pretty careful with the kids, but you never know. And I can't tell Jeff to watch himself or anything like that. He'd get mad and wouldn't listen. His father already thinks I'm making him into a mama's boy. What does he expect? He's never around. I have to be both mother and father to him.

Jeff's yawning. He must be getting tired. They're all getting tired. They're shooting off four or five at a time now. I don't see Marilyn and Patti. Jay and Ted and Ange and Longie are still here, so the girls must be inside. Robert's hunched over in his lawn chair. It looks like he's sleeping. I wonder if he's drunk. Dorie's chatting to Ange and Ted, and Virginia's laughing and clapping after every whoosh or bang. She's been doing that all night. I wish I had her energy and enthusiasm. People sometimes think we're sisters. Probably because we both have red hair.

"Okay, that's it. I'm tired." "What about these over here, Uncle?" "Ask your mom if you can take those home." "Mom, can I take these home? Can I?" "I suppose so, if there aren't too many." Everyone except Robert and Longie gets up at once. Dorie lights up a cigarette, Ted yawns and stretches, and Jay starts clearing the paper plates, plastic glasses and paper napkins from the picnic table. "Do you want to save any of this plasticware?" "No, just throw it all out." "Ted, could you grab these beer cans and throw them away please?" I stand up too quickly and feel a little dizzy. I hope I didn't drink too much wine. "C'mon kids, we're going upstairs. Bobby, Bo, Jeff, c'mon." I take the empty bowl of potato salad I made. I don't want to forget the bowl. I'm not dizzy anymore, just tired.

We climb the outside stairs to the deck and into the kitchen. Jay starts putting stuff away, and I move to the sink to wash my salad bowl. Ange pours herself another glass of wine. "Leave all this stuff: we'll do it later. Right now, I want everyone to see how we've decorated Babe's den. C'mon, down the stairs." I don't see Jeff in the kitchen. I thought he was right behind me. "Where's Jeff?" "He's on the couch in the living room, watching TV. He'll be fine. C'mon everyone. Down the stairs, let's go." "Okay, we're going down the stairs," says Longie. "Babe, let's see this new den."

I would call it more of a recreation room than a den. I'd sure like to do something with our basement. Finish it at least. Babe and Virginia love Las Vegas, and Virginia has decorated the den with all kinds of ornaments from the casinos. There's a big neon sign with The Sands in red cursive hanging on the wall over the bar. Near the bar there are two plastic pink flamingos that light up as Virginia flips a switch. Babe's table where he plays poker is covered with a green felt cloth that says Golden Nugget, just like the real thing. There are small folding tables surrounding the big table, with ashtrays and coasters from The Sands, The Dunes, The Riviera, The Tropicana, The Flamingo and The Thunderbird. There's even a slot machine in the corner, just like my cousin Florence and I used to play in Elko. "Most of this stuff was comp," Virginia said. "Not most. Some." "What does 'comp' mean?" "Complimentary. They give you things so you'll come back and lose even more money, ain't that right Babe?" explains Longie. The pink flamingo lights and the neon give the room a funny look.

Babe moves behind the bar. "Anyone want a nightcap? I've got booze, beer, wine and pop. Robert?" "I'll have a little whisky." "Ted? Longie?" "I'll have a beer." "I'll have some wine." "I'll have some wine too," says Ange. My mouth is dry. "I'd like a ginger ale." "Sure Frances." Robert moves over to the record player and fools with it for a while. The rock-and-roll stops, and then a loud scratch, and then Frank Sinatra starts up. "Sorry girls," Robert says to Patti and Marilyn, "but this is for your Aunt Dorie." He glides over to her, puts his arm around her, and they start dancing. Patti and Marilyn scrunch up their faces, and then disappear into another room. Ted and

Jay start dancing too. They're good dancers. Virginia walks into the middle of the room and starts swaying back and forth. "C'mon Babe," she shouts. He sets my ginger ale down on the bar and joins her. Even Longie and Ange join the party. They're holding each other and pivoting around and around on his artificial leg. I sit up on a barstool. I'm glad Babe put ice in my pop.

FATHER

I don't want to go to the office today and see that bastard Giadone Jr. give me the eye. When are you going to close a deal Frank? Look at the board. He won't say nothing to my face, but I can tell what's he thinking, that spineless bastard. I can't make a deal because Pueblo's like a sinking ship: everybody's getting out as fast as they can. Like rats, like rats. Who'm I gonna sell to? He wouldn't even give me a new phone book, the son of a bitch. How petty is that? Everyone else got new phone books on their desk except me. And when I confronted him, I did it in a nice way, I asked him where my new phone book was, he just said they didn't have enough to go around. Didn't have enough to go around. That petty son of a bitch. His father was okay, but not the son, not the son. The son's a petty son of a bitch.

I can't stay home: I got to at least pretend like I'm making calls. And fat Frances and her dopey son are here, puttering around all day. I wish that kid would get a summer job. The question mark. I was working when I was fourteen. Hell, I was selling wine when I was twelve. Helping out the family. That boy don't do nothing but mope around the house and read. I wish Frances would get a summer job too, get her out of the house, get out of my life. The house is already hot, it's going to be a scorcher today. I gotta get out of here. I got to get out of here. "I'm going to work, that's where I'm going. I'll be home when I'm home."

It's too early to go to the Legion Hall or the Branch Inn. Maybe I'll drive around, go to the old neighborhood. Goddamn you car, goddamn you, you're too fucking hot car, too fucking hot. It's like an oven, this car. And I can't afford a new one, with air-conditioning. JoJo's got a nice car, a Lincoln. And Tommy the Rock gets a new Cadillac every couple of years. And I'm stuck with this nine-year-old Pontiac Star Chief hand-me-down piece of junk. Maybe I should take Big Red, tell Frances I have a client. I'm already sweating here. Maybe I'll go to the library and read the *Denver Post*. At least it's cool in there. God damn it's hot.

Hurry up, hurry up. Look at all this traffic. I'm living on a highway, living on a highway. The steering wheel's burning my hands. Where are all these people going? It's ten o'clock in the morning, where are they going? All these kids with cars. There are more cars than people in this country, more cars than people. "Stay home, goddamn it, stay home." What are you looking at, you buttana? Kids and women, stay home and stop wasting gas. That's what's wrong with this country: too many cars and too many women who don't stay home. Clean your houses. Turn green you fucking light turn green.

I don't want to go to the library. I'm tired of reading the paper. I'm tired of the news. It's always the same: Watergate Watergate Watergate. Of course he's guilty, everyone lies to get into office and then they lie to stay in office. They're all bastards, Democrats and Republicans, they're all the same. Nixon just got caught, that's all, he just got caught. That John Dean's a sneaky son of a bitch. But they're all sneaky sons of bitches: Mitchell, Liddy, Halderman, Erlichman, Anglo bastards. Germans. I'm sick of them. And people are surprised. I'm not surprised. I know how the world works: everyone's a cheating bastard. They just got caught. It's historical, sure it's historical. How many times has something like this happened and we didn't hear about it? Kennedy, JFK was fucking Marilyn Monroe, Marilyn Monroe and all those other women. And Roosevelt had his Lucy Mercer. Everyone sneaks around. Everyone lies. You can't trust anybody. What do I want to read about those bastards for? I know it already, I'm not stupid, I know it.

I wonder what's happening here at the fairgrounds. Are they having a circus maybe or something? I don't know. It's so fucking hot. It's too hot to drive down to Box Elder and the old neighborhood. I'll go to the library. It'll be cool and I'll be able to kill an hour, maybe read *Time* or *Look*. Then back home for lunch. I think I have six dollars. I can hit the Branch Inn or the Legion this afternoon for a couple of beers.

What time is it? Twelve thirty. I must have dozed off a little. I'm hungry. Maybe I'll go get a McDonald's hamburger or something instead of going home. I can get a hamburger and then head over to the Legion for a couple of beers. They have Budweiser in the tall necks. I don't want to go all the way over to the Branch Inn in this heat. I don't want to see anybody I know either. I just want to sit someplace cool, drink my beer, relax. I don't want to see nobody.

Maybe I'll go to the bowling alley. I can have a sandwich and a beer cheap there, and it'll be cool. There won't be too many people there in the day, and I'll stay in the lounge so it won't be too noisy. The bowling alley's a nice place. They got those comfortable chairs in the lounge and you can sit for two, three hours and no one bothers you. It's better than the movies. Who's going to pay three dollars to see that crap they put on the screen? *Earthquake, The Burning Tower,* who wants to see that crap? I don't even want to see *The Godfather.* He's a traitor, that Coppola, a goddamn traitor. Every time we see an Italian in the movies he belongs to the mafia. I'm so sick of it. It really burns me up. One time, I'd like to see an Italian who does something good. One time. And now they're making *The Godfather II.* Goddamn Italians. When you going to wake up! The Anglos eat that stuff up. When you going to wake up!

I really snuffed that down. This beer's nice and cold too. I wish they'd given me more potato chips. This place is deserted, a couple of high school kids and a family. I don't know how this joint stays in business. I went bowling once, with Babe. I didn't really go for it. We took a couple of girls. This was just after the war. We took the trolley to Bessemer and after we dropped the girls off it was late, so we had to walk back from Mineral Palace Park. I didn't get nothing that night, not even a kiss. Babe's a good bowler. He likes games. I like to strap, that's the only game I like.

I got what, four dollars left? Three-fifty? Maybe I could borrow some money from Chuck. What time is it? Only one-fifteen. I got money for two more beers, three if I don't leave a tip. I got some change in the car. I'll get another beer and watch the people bowl.

MOTHER

I feel his heartbeat next to me and I feel so important. So unimportant too. Look at his little eyes, his tiny little mouth. And his hands, those darling little fingers. Now I know what Ma went through. I wish she could be here to see this. He's nuzzling me, looking for my breast. He needs me so. I'll do anything for him. Anything. He's so beautiful. He's the most beautiful thing I've ever seen.

Joe wants to name him George, or John, or Mark, but I don't like those names. I've always liked the name Jeff. He looks like a Jeff to me. Jeff DeShell. Hello there, little Jeff DeShell. I'm Frances DeShell, your mother. Your father, Joe DeShell, will be here soon. He wasn't in the waiting room. The nurse said she called him at home and he's coming right down. I don't blame him, he'd been waiting a while. It was a quick delivery too. It hurt like the dickens, but it was quick. You wanted to come out, little Jeff, you wanted to come out to play. I can't tell if he's looking at me or not. Joe will be happy he's a boy. I am too. Boys seem to have it easier in the world.

His head sure is big. The rest of him is skinny and long, almost too skinny to hold up that big head. The nurse told me I'd have to support it when I held him. The doctor said he was healthy, so I guess he is. He's not fussing much. They said I could hold him until his father came in, but then I'd have to let them take him so I could get some rest. I'm hoping Joe doesn't come for a while. I'd like to hold him for a long time.

He looks like my father a little bit. He looks like a baby mostly, so red and soft, but there's something about his cheeks and around his eyes that remind me of Pa. I'm going to have to call my family. I know Joe won't do it. Jeff's eyes are closing. He's yawning. He must be sleepy. He's so beautiful. Oh dear, I'm yawning too. I guess I'm sleepy as well. And sore, especially down there and in my rear end.

February 16th. Sixteen candles, happy birthday, happy birthday baby, for I love you so. I like that song. "Sixteen candles, happy birthday baby..." "Helloooooooo. Can we come in?" It's Virginia. I nod and smile. She tiptoes in, followed by Jay and Ted. Ted is holding a big bunch of flowers and Jay is carrying a brightly wrapped package. Oh my. "Congratulations, Frances, congratulations. We brought you some flowers." "Thank you, thank you." "Ted and I brought this. For the baby. It's a baby blanket. From Chatham. They're a good company, Frances, very high quality." "Oh dear. Thank you very much." "I'll just set it down here." Virginia leans over the bed. "Let me look at him, let me get an eyeful. Oh, he's so cute. Frances, he is a little darlin'. Where's his daddy? Has Joe seen him yet?" I don't say anything, and Virginia says under her breath, "You'd think he'd be here to see his first child being born. You'd think he'd be here for that." He'll be here soon. Jeff opens his eyes and yawns again. "He's such a little darlin'. Babe and I bought him a giant teddy bear. It's down in the car. I didn't want to bring it up and scare the poor thing on his first day."

Jeff yawns again and closes his eyes tight, making tiny wrinkles around his eyes. His right arm twitches up and down up and down, then relaxes. His legs kick, and his mouth opens

146

and closes, almost like a little fish. He's so small and vulnerable. I can't get over how lovely he is.

"There he is, there's his daddy." "Congratulations, Joe, congratulations!" "Thanks Ted." "How's it feel to be a father?" "Pretty good, pretty good. Let me see him. Hold him up, Frances, hold up my son." I hold him out a little bit, careful to prop up his head. "He looks good, he looks good." "Hold him, Joe." "I don't want to hold him now, I'll hold him later. I'll hold him later." I pull Jeff back to my body. "Everything okay? Everything turn out all right?" A nurse walks in the room and answers. "Everything turned out fine. Your wife and son are healthy. It was a rapid delivery. I'm sorry, but you'll all have to leave now. Mother and baby need their rest. Visiting hours are tomorrow two to four. Please." As everyone gets ready to leave, she turns back to me and says, "I'll give you five more minutes, but you need your rest."

I watch him sleep. He's so beautiful. And so small. His arm is twitching again. I wonder if he's dreaming now. What are your dreams, little Jeff DeShell? What will you be when you grow up? I touch the top of his head with my palm. His skin is smooth and cool, and his skull feels soft. I put my finger on his forehead and trace his nose, his lips and down to his chin. He grimaces, and his head turns slightly. My son. My beautiful son.

Can he feel how much I love him? Does he know how happy he's made me? Will he ever understand that he means everything to me? I don't believe I've ever been this happy before. It makes me a little scared. I don't know what I'd do if anything happened to him. I really don't.

FATHER

I'm sitting at this bar. It looks like Gus' or Veteran's Tavern, but classy. I'm having a beer, and this nice-looking lady walks up to me and asks if I have a cigarette. She's beautiful, with long blond hair and big dark eyes, a real figa. I feel hard immediately. I give her a cigarette, and light it, and she puts her hand on mine. "You're a good-looking man," she says. I can see her brown nipples through the top of her dress. She reminds me of Rita Hayworth in *Gilda*. I saw that at the Chief Theater when I came back from the war. "Thank you," I say. "Can I buy you a drink?" What? What's that? Where am I? It's dark, and I'm lying down. I look up and see a gray rectangle above me. The downstairs window. I smell laundry soap. God damn it. I'm in my bed in the basement. I'm not in a bar. Rita Hayworth doesn't want to go to bed with me. I hear Christmas music above.

Everything's against me. I can't even enjoy a dream.

I want to go back to sleep. I'm tired of thinking. I'm tired of fighting the world. I need some goddamn peace. I never liked Rita Hayworth that much. She was always too Anglo for me. I like strapping the dark ones, like Anna Magnini, or Ida Lupino in *The Man I Love*. Or Jennifer Jones in *Duel in the Sun*. I'd really like to strap that buttana. I saw *Duel in the Sun* at the

148

Chief too. In 1947? Or '46? I don't fucking know. Movies were a quarter. They knew how to make movies then, that's for goddamn sure. I haven't been to a movie in ten years: what do I want to pay five dollars to see crap for? That music's getting louder. "Turn it down!" I hate fucking Christmas music. I hate fucking Christmas. "TURN IT FUCKING DOWN!" I lost my mother at Christmas. I remember the Christmas day, two weeks after my mother died. Aunt Filomena, my father's sister, sent some toy trucks from New York, and me and Babe played with them until he started crying. My father made us go to mass and I hated those songs and I hated all those people in their nice clothes and fancy hats. My father died at Christmas too, ten years later.

Jeff's home. That's why Frances thinks she can ignore me. Two against one, all the time. He acts like it's a favor to come see his folks. Big favor. He can't wait to go back to Boulder. He barely talks to us while he's here. He just mopes around, or buries his head in a book, or listens to that goddamn jungle music. He's got his mother fooled. She thinks the sun rises and sets with that boy. God I wish he was a better son. What a disappointment he turned out to be. What a disappointment.

I need more sleep. I need to get the fuck out of this racist town. Find me a new family, start the fuck over somewhere else, wipe the slate clean. I need a new wife, a new job, some sons that will give me grandchildren, carry my name to the next century. Not my son, he's too goddamn mopey to do anything. I'm trapped. Trapped in a bad marriage, trapped in a dead-end job, trapped with a son I can't stand, trapped in the racist town of Pueblo Colorado, where I can't get a break, trapped trapped trapped. I hate my fucking life. Thank you God. Christmas. What have you done for me, God, what have you done for me?

149

I need to urinate. I sit up and pull the light switch. Where's my robe? Sleeping in the basement like an animal. It's cold down here. Where's my other slipper? Goddamn it, it's under the bed. Nothing goes right for me, nothing. I'm going to turn that fucking Christmas music off when I get upstairs. I need my sleep.

Who the fuck they think I am, exiled to the basement? I'm the man of the house, the king of the castle, and I sleep downstairs like an animal. There they are, sitting in the living room, two against one, two against one. "What are you looking at? Turn that goddamn TV down. I need my sleep. Turn it off now! And don't wrap no present for me, I don't want nothing. I lost my mother at Christmas. I hate fucking Christmas." They just sit there and look at me. "What are you looking at?" I cross the room and switch off the television. I can feel their eyes on my back as I move toward the bathroom.

I flush the toilet and start to make water. I look down at my tool in the harsh light: unused, weak, old. I deserve better than this. I deserve someone like Anna Magnini, or some nice Italian wench who doesn't speak English and straps like a whore. Not a fat Anglo wife and mopey son. He's got no moxie, no initiative. And his mother just sits there like a bump on a log. No wonder I had to shop around. How I got stuck with those two I'll never know. I finish and close my robe with my belt. My robe's all ratty and torn, but I don't give a goddamn. I like what I am.

I reach to wash my hands and knock the toothpaste onto the floor. "Fuck! You goddamn thing, come here!" Nothing goes right for me, I swear to fucking God. I pick the tube up and slam it down on the back of the sink. It sticks to my hand as I move it away and drops to the floor again. "MOTHERFUCKER! GODDAMN FUCKING TOOTHPASTE

FUCK!" I'll leave it on the floor. Let someone do something for me for a change. I'm tired of doing everything for everybody. I'm sick of everyone. I'm sick of life.

As I finish washing my hands, I hear music coming from the living room. I turned that goddamn thing off. I'll show them. I'll show them to treat me like an animal. I'll show them to give me some respect. I fling open the door and march out to the living room. "I told you to turn that off. I don't care if it's Christmas, I lost my mother at Christmas. Turn that crap off. I said TURN THAT CRAP OFF!" They both just sit there motionless, staring at me, Frances in her chair and Jeff on the couch. Two against one, all the time, two against one. The whole world is against me. I want to slap that look off both their faces. "Turn that television off Frances, before I break it. And then I'll break you." Jeff stands up. I'd like to punch him right in the face. I'd like to punch them both. Frances starts to sing with the music. Her voice is loud and shrill. Jeff starts singing too. I'll show them, I'll break that fucking TV. I move towards the television but Jeff steps in my way. "Get out of my way! I said get out of my way!" He doesn't move. I can see the hate in his eyes. God I'd like to punch him in the mouth. One punch, one punch. I'll go to jail, I don't care. One fucking punch. Frances' voice is getting louder and higher. She sounds nuts. I'll show them. I move to the left corner of the room, take the Christmas tree in my right hand, and slam it to the floor. That shut them up. That shut them up good. I go back downstairs. I need my sleep.

FATHER

MOTHER

I'm getting married tomorrow. New Year's Eve, 1957. Joe says we'll save money on taxes this year, and I guess that's true.

I hope this is the right thing to do. It feels like the right thing. I'm not getting any younger, and Joe makes me laugh. I guess I love him. I like his tanned skin and dark curly hair, and the way he holds me and kisses me. I wonder where he is now. He said he was going to a movie, but I haven't heard him come back yet. I wish he were kissing me now. And he dresses so well, like a real gentleman. Pa doesn't like him much, doesn't trust him. Neither does my brother. They both wonder why we're not having a church wedding, and why we decided to go all the way to Santa Barbara to get married, in front of a JP, alone, with no family or best man or maid of honor or anything. When I told them we're going to Hawaii for our honeymoon, Pa just cleared his throat and Lowell didn't say anything. It was almost like I could hear them frowning over the telephone.

Maybe they're right. When I was a little girl, I always thought I'd have a big church wedding, with lots of flowers, a big white cake, and all my girlfriends in red satin dresses. When I went to college in Hannibal, and when I started teaching, I thought I'd have a smaller wedding with my family and a few friends in a chapel in the woods, someplace quiet, secluded and nice. By the time I got to Fulton I wasn't sure I'd get married at all. Then I met Mr. Damasio, and I thought, just for a little while, that we'd run away to get married, maybe to Europe or New York or someplace like that. That didn't work. Only one of us ran away. I'm not saying this is my last chance or anything, but all my friends and cousins, Florence, Nadine, Lela, Laura, Sarabell, even Mary Jane McCleery, have husbands, and all have children except Lela and Mary Jane, and Mary Jane's pregnant. I don't want to be an old maid. I want to have kids. I'm thirty-six and not getting any younger.

I wonder what tomorrow will be like. We have to be at the courthouse at three thirty, and then we're going to a fancy restaurant afterwards. I know it's not going to be like my brother's wedding, but it would be nice to have my dad and Lowell here, and a few friends, like Flo or Lela. And some flowers, some lilies or azaleas. Joe said he didn't want a big production. I hope he'll at least buy me a corsage. He's been married before. Joe will look handsome, I'm sure. I bought a new dress, a pretty cream colored one with pale blue violets, and new stockings, and the high heels I bought last year at the Fair department store in Chicago are in good shape because I hardly ever wear them. Flo, Lela and Laura all chipped in and sent me a new nightgown and slip. I wonder if someone will take our picture at the courthouse. I wonder if they'll play the wedding march.

Was that his door? No. The day after tomorrow we'll get on a ship to go to Hawaii. At least I'm hoping we will. Sometimes I can't believe it's really going to happen. I have some money saved, and my dad gave us five hundred dollars as a wedding present. Joe said he'd get the rest from his sisters. Santa Barbara's so pretty; Hawaii must be even prettier. We went to the boardwalk this afternoon and looked out at the Pacific Ocean. I imagine Hawaii will be all different kinds of green, and the water will be blue blue blue, bluer than it is here. I've never been on a ship on the ocean before. I hope I don't get seasick.

I wish Ma were here. If she were still alive, I'd try to get Joe to let us have a bigger wedding, with flowers and cake and guests, just so Ma could see her only daughter getting married off. Finally. We never talked that much, but I'd like to visit with her tonight. I don't know what I'd say, but it would be fine if she were sitting over there in the chair, maybe drinking a glass of lemonade, and me knowing she was happy for me, and proud of me too. Oh dear, I don't know why I'm thinking such silly thoughts.

I'm having a hard time falling asleep. I must be all bothered, because usually I'm asleep as soon as my head hits the pillow. It's almost twelve-thirty. I still haven't heard him come back. He wanted to share a room, said it would be cheaper, but I told him that we weren't married yet and that he shouldn't see me the day of the wedding anyway. I think that made him mad. I'm not a Miss Prude, we practically shared a room for a night in Reno on the way out here, but I just thought having separate rooms for a couple of nights before the wedding would be more pleasant. Maybe I was wrong.

This is the last night I'll have the whole bed to myself. That will sure be different. I'll have to change my name too. Mrs. Joseph DeShell. Mrs. Joseph DeShell. I'll have to get used to that.

We'll move to Pueblo after our honeymoon. I'd rather live someplace nicer, like California, but Joe wants to be close to his family, and so that's where we'll live. His brother is pleasant, but I'm not sure his sisters like me. I suppose they think

I'm not good enough for Joe, or maybe they want him to marry someone younger. Or someone Italian. I don't know. I'm not going to worry about them. I'm getting married today.

FATHER

There they are, there they are. Look at them, all dressed up in their Indian costumes and Mexican hats. Show-offs. Beat that drum, beat that drum you sons of bitches. We've got our own orchestra, a small marching band. Columbus was a Killer. We Won't Celebrate Genocide. Columbus is the Hitler of America! Fuck them, the Hitler of America. How stupid, how stupid. How'd they like it if we stopped them from celebrating Cinco de Mayo? What about Montezuma and human sacrifice?

I blame the Italians. I've been telling them for years, the Knights of Columbus, Sons of Italy, La Famiglia Italiana, we've got to pay attention, we've got to stand up for our rights. We're not the "in" minority, we're not the Mexicans, blacks or women, and so no one's going to help us. We've got to stand up for ourselves. We've been discriminated against for hundreds of years, and nobody knows our story. We get *The Godfather*, *The Sopranos* and all that John Gotti crap, but nobody knows how we can't get jobs, how we can't be heard, how we're stereotyped by the media. Look at Cuomo. He answered my letter once when he was governor of New York. He didn't want to run for president because he knew all the mafia questions he'd have to answer. And this racist town of Pueblo Colorado, where I can't even get my letter to the editor published. Ten years ago, fifteen years ago, they published my letter, and nothing since. I asked that editor, the city editor, that young punk from Harvard, and he said they couldn't read my writing. But even when Frances copied it out carefully, they still didn't print it. And now the publisher, Rawlings, wants to build a library, that bastard. A million dollars for a library, but he won't print my goddamn articles. I hate that son of a bitch. You talk about freedom of the press in Russia or China, what about freedom of the press in Pueblo Colorado? What about our civil rights, the right to peaceful assembly? But I blame the Italians. They wouldn't listen to me. And now here we are, fighting with a bunch of Indians and Mexicans who don't even live here, trying to march down the street.

It's starting to rain. I'm glad I brought my hat. There's Councilman Santarelli, a real phony. A phony Italian. An Uncle Tom Italian. I asked him to put me on the civil rights commission, I asked him to put me on the equal housing commission, I asked him to put me on the regional development commission, but he won't put me on nothing. He's worried that I might say something to upset the Anglo establishment. Hell yes I want to upset the Anglo establishment. I want to call attention to this racist town. He wouldn't even nominate me for dogcatcher, that phony bastard.

The orchestra starts playing Italian music, and we're moving. About time. I guess Jo Jo ain't coming. Seventy-five years old and he still works everyday, from noon until midnight, serving drinks and making macaroni. It keeps him young. He told me he probably wouldn't come. "Frank, if I come, I'll get so goddamn mad I'll bust a couple of those knuckleheads with a baseball bat, and I'll end up in Florence." Listen to them yell. Why don't you leave us alone? "Leave us alone, goddamn

157

it. We're not doing anything to you! Oh yeah, whatta about Montezuma? What about human sacrifice?" Read your history you stupid Mexican, or Indian, or whatever the fuck you are. "Hello there, Mr. Koncilja. How are you doing? Look at those mokes over there. I thought there'd be more of us, you know Mr. Koncilja? It's raining, but it's like I told the lodge, we're a forgotten minority, we're not the Mexicans, blacks or women, and we gotta stand up for our rights. You were there, you heard me. Yeah." That Joe Koncilja's a nice guy. He and his brother Jimmy, lawyers, bought up all of South Union and the train depot, turned it around. That's where they work, and they bought it up and made it nice. When I was in real estate, I couldn't give that property away, now it's a million dollar block.

"What are you looking at? What? What did you say? We have a right to march, a right to have our parade. Read the Constitution. What if we tried to stop you from celebrating Cinco de Mayo? Or Fiesta Days at the fair? Yeah, I'm an old man. What? Fuck you too! I'm not going to calm down. Did you hear what he called me? Fuck you too." He called me a motherfucking wop. That's a racial slur. If I called him an ignorant savage, I'd probably get arrested. Yeah, I'm a wop, I'm a wop all right, a wop of Michelangelo and Leonardo da Vinci, a wop of Caruso and all those other opera singers, while all you can do is howl and beat that stupid drum. What was that guy's name, the guy with the Lone Ranger? Tonto. "How Tonto, how!"

The guy ducks under the yellow police tape and rushes me. Joe Koncilja pulls me back, and a couple of paisans, one big and one not so big, but wiry and mean looking, step in front. The Indian, or Mexican or whatever stops, but then lunges, and as he's being held by the paisans, spits at me. The little paisan decks him, and his whole tribe hops over the barricades to go after the paisans. One cop quickly rides his bicycle to cut the Indians off, and a bunch of other cops jump in. The parade stops, and I feel guys pushing me from the back, trying to get into it with the Indians. The music's still playing and everyone's yelling. I shout "How Tonto, how Tonto" a couple of times, but stay back, close to Joe Koncilja the lawyer. There are more and more cops, a couple on horses, and they soon separate the two lines. They tell us to move on. We start up again.

"Yeah, I'm okay. Thanks for asking Joe." He points to the lapel of my jacket. There's some saliva and snot where the fucking Indian spit on me. He hands me his handkerchief, and I clean myself up. That fucking slob. To spit on an old man, what kind of thing is that? No respect. Barbarians. Savages. "You ain't going to want this back, are you Joe?" He shakes his head. I stuff it in my pocket and keep my eyes open for a garbage can.

MOTHER

"Well come on in, come on in. You must be Frances." "And you must be John." "That's right. You can call me Babe. This is my wife, Virginia. Let me take your coat, Frances. How you doing, Frank?" "Call me Joe, call me Joe." Babe's handsome like Joe, only taller. His forehead is a little broader. He's got a kind face. I like Virginia's red hair, all pushed up high like that. She's wearing a nice pale green dress. Her face is almost as red as her hair. "Happy Thanksgiving Frances. Come in and sit down. Frank. Happy Thanksgiving." "Joe. Call me Joe." "It's Joe today, huh? Okay, happy Thanksgiving Joe." Joe gives her a hateful look I've never seen before. Oh my. I hope she didn't see it. "I have to use your restroom," he says. "You know where it is, Joe."

Babe hangs my coat and Virginia takes my arm and leads me into the living room, where two of Joe's sisters are sitting on the couch, and the young one is smoking in an armchair near the window. Dorie's the young one, then Dolly, then Josephine and then Angela. Or is it Josephine, then Dolly and then Angela? I can't keep them straight. "Frances Patterson, this is Josephine Ciavonne," she nods and smiles, "Ange Vadnal," slight nod, no smile "and Doris Fruscella," a mean little smile, somewhat like Joe's. "Dolly is with the kids in the den. These are Joe's and Babe's sisters. The husbands are out in the garage, doing God knows what. Please, sit." Dorie's wearing a short black dress and hose, and red high heel shoes. She looks like she's dressed for a nightclub. Ange has a brown knit dress and brown flat shoes and Josephine's wearing an expensive-looking red and white skirt suit, stockings and black flats. "Did you offer Frances something to drink?" "Not yet. I was trying to get her comfortable. Jesus Christ." "Don't talk to me like that." "Well don't stick your nose in my business. I know how to treat my guests. Your family." "Then offer her something to drink, god-damn it." "I will. Don't you worry about it." "I won't." "Good." Oh dear. I don't want to be any trouble. I look down at my hands. I see one of my fingernails is a little chipped.

"Would you like something to drink, Frances? We have beer and wine, and Babe will make you a cocktail if you'd like." "Oh no, I'm fine." "Some lemonade? Ice tea? Water?" I should take something. I don't want to be impolite and I like ice tea. "I'd like some ice tea please." "Coming right up." Dorie leans over towards me. "Do you smoke Frances? Would you like a cigarette?" "No, no, I have my own, thank you." "Do you want me to move the ashtray closer?" "No, I'm not going to smoke just yet. Thank you, though."

"You're from Iowa, is that right?" Josephine asks. I turn back toward the couch. "No, I'm from Illinois." "Oh, Illinois. That's nice. She's from Illinois, Ange." "Illinois, huh? How long have you been here in Colorado?" "I've been in Greeley two years. At the teacher's college there. That's where I met Joe. Before that I taught in Elko Nevada." "Have you ever been to Pueblo before?" "No. This is my first time." "How do you like Pueblo?" "It seems very nice. I haven't had the chance to see much, though. I've only been here a day and a half." "Where are you staying, Frances?" "I'm staying at the YWCA. It's clean and comfortable, and not very expensive. They give you little bars of soap." "The YMCA, where's that at?" "It's that big building on Santa Fe. Santa Fe and Eighth. You know, Ange, the one with the red tile roof." "I didn't know it was a hotel." "It's not exactly a hotel. It's more of a woman's dormitory, or residence hall. It's like a boarding house." "It's like a boarding house, huh. Hmmm." No one says anything for a while. I look down at my hands again, then back up at the couch. Ange takes a drink from an orange tumbler as Josephine smiles at me. I see Dorie out of the corner of my eye putting out her cigarette in the ashtray. I wonder where Joe and Babe went.

"We hear you and Frank are going to get married. That's so nice. We're happy for you." "Thank you." "We're very glad you could come to the dinner tonight. It was Virginia's idea to get us all together for Thanksgiving, to give us all a chance to get to know you before the wedding. Frank hasn't told us much. He says that after you get married you're coming back to Pueblo to live. Is that right?" "I believe so. I've applied to the school district for next fall, and I should know soon whether I can start then or have to wait another year." We're going to get married in Hawaii, but I don't know if I should tell them that. I don't want to brag. "That's nice, Frances, that's really nice. Do you like being a school teacher?" "I enjoy it very much. I like being around children." "Would you like to have children, Frances? Children of your own?" "Yes, of course. Yes I would. You all have children, right?" "I don't. I'm not married." Oh no, I hope I haven't offended Dorie. "Oh, I'm sorry. I didn't mean anything." "I'm not sorry. I like living alone." She lights up a cigarette, "I have a dog, I don't need a husband," and starts to laugh. Josephine cuts her off. "I have a son, Mike, who's five and a daughter, Pattie, who's eight. Ange has a son, Bobby, who's seven and a daughter, Marilyn, four. Dolly has a daughter, Karen, who's six. No, seven. You'll meet them soon. Virginia and Babe don't have children yet." "Does Frank like children?" Ange asks. "How do I know?" says Josephine. "I can't imagine Frank as a father," says Dorie. "Frank would make a good father. Babe would too. You don't know what you're talking about," Josephine says. I have a hard time thinking of Joe when they say Frank. I didn't know people knew him as Frank. Joe said he wanted a son, and I really want to have children too. I'm not getting any younger. I think he'll make a good father. He can be so funny sometimes. These questions are a little personal. "This would be the perfect thing for Frank. I feel sorry for him. He's had a hard time lately. It would be a good thing for him to settle down and have children. He deserves happiness." Josephine looks at me and gives me a nice smile. I'm not sure what to think.

The other sister, Dolly, walks in from the kitchen. She's wearing a vanilla cable-knit sweater and a yellow and gray wool skirt. She looks like she must be hot. Dorie and Josephine seem to care more about clothes than Ange or Dolly. I hope they think I'm dressed nicely. She says, "Hello Frances, I'm Dolly," and hands me one of those orange tumblers. "Virginia asked me to bring this in to you while she's checking the turkey. Do you take sugar or lemon?" "No, just plain will be fine. Thank you." "You're welcome. How do you like Pueblo, Frances? Have you been here before?" "We asked her that already," Ange says from the couch. "She likes it fine and she's never been here before." "How could I know that, Ange? I was with the kids. I'm sorry, Frances. So you like Pueblo?" "I haven't seen much, but I like what little I've seen."

FATHER

"C'mon Frances, get ready. Do you know where I'm taking you? I don't know if they'll let me come in the booth with you, but I'll be right there. C'mon." I wish there was something someone could do to stop this. She's really going downhill, she's going downhill fast. "We got to get your coat on." It's not warm in here, and they don't even put a sweater on her. I told them I was taking her out: you'd think they'd have her coat on her and ready to go. She should say something too. She never complains. Never says "I'm cold" or "I have to go to the bathroom." Jesus God, this is hard on me. It wasn't supposed to be like this. I have my civil rights work, my Italian civil rights campaign, and now I have to be a caregiver. I'm an old man. It's not fair.

I go to her closet to get her coat. Her roommate is lying down with her back toward the door and her face toward the window. She's been in here ten years. Ten years with the Alzheimer's. God, I hope Frances doesn't stay in here ten years. I hope to God she gets better. I look around the room. We had to put a bed with short legs in here because she fell out a couple of times. A bed, a closet, a nightstand. That's what she has. I should put a TV in here. She likes to watch those old shows like *I Love Lucy* and the Beaver show. That'll cost some money, though. I'm already paying almost four thousand a month. Four thousand for what? For basic room and board. She's not getting any help. She's not getting any therapy. Look at her arm, look how thin and weak it looks. Like a skeleton's. She's been out of the cast almost three weeks and that arm still looks like that. What therapy? What therapy I ask you? A TV would cost a lot. Maybe I'll do it though.

These labels on everything—light, bed, closet, bathroom—I don't know what goddamn good they do. I don't know how much she reads. She used to read the paper forwards and back, used to x-ray the goddamn paper. She'd sit in that chair for an hour at least, humming to herself, reading every page, even the ads. Here's her coat. I have to put nametags on everything, even her breast prosthesis, or else they disappear. Mrs. Nance tells me it's the other patients who take things, but they're just covering their asses. If they'd pay these people more, I mean the foot soldiers who do all the work, who change and bathe these old people, then they wouldn't have to take the clothes and other stuff. Her prosthesis was missing for almost a month. A hundred and fifty dollar prosthesis, the size of a football, and they couldn't find it. Who would steal a thing like that? I said to them, "What are you people doing? Why would someone take a breast prosthesis? You can't sell the goddamn thing." And they said to me that it wasn't stolen, it was just "missing." Missing. I got on 'em. Every day I'd ask them, "Where's her prosthesis? Did you find her prosthesis?" I'm not making any friends here. Finally they found it. One of the nurses' aides misplaced it with one of the other ladies' things. You got to get on these people here. You got to say, "Did you brush her teeth? Did she go to the bathroom? Put a coat on her." I'm not popular. I got to be this way. Think about all these old people who don't have no one to care for them, no one to watch out and see if they're getting cleaned up, if they're getting the right medicine, if their prosthesis and stuff isn't stolen. No one here likes to see me coming. But I like what I am.

"Frances. Come here. Before we get in the car, you need to write out the names of who you're going to vote for and then sign it, in case they don't let me in the booth with you. Okay, here's a pen, and here's a paper, you can sit right here, and write out these names, hold the pen, Frances, hold the pen, like that, hold the pen right, like that damn it, hold the pen right and trace out these names, Al Gore and Curtis Imrie. A, L, A, L. God damn it, Frances, can't you write anymore? I'll write it on this piece of paper, you trace it, okay. Watch. Watch! A-L G-O-R-E. Okay? C-U-R-T-I-S I-M-R-I-E. Now trace it. Trace it goddamn it. What is wrong with you? Here, let me do it, and you sign your name. Can you do that? There. You just sign your name. Hold the pen. Pick up the pen and hold it right. There. Now sign your name. Hold the pen right and sign your name. SIGN YOUR NAME GODDAMN IT!"

"Hello there. My name is Joseph DeShell, and this is my wife Frances DeShell. We're here to vote. My wife had a stroke. She's mentally competent, but can't speak that good any more. She might need some help with the machines. I *can* go in and help her, huh? Okay, thank you."

That election lady is looking at us kind of funny. I don't give a damn. "C'mon Frances, c'mon. Sign your name. Hold the pen and sign your name." She has trouble holding the pen. She can't coordinate herself anymore. "C'mon Frances. Here, let me help you. Can I help her? Here Frances, hold the pen and sign your name. That's it. Good. I'll print her name underneath. There. C'mon Frances, take your ballot and let's go over here."

166

These new machines are so damn complicated. I like the old ways, those big booths with the curtains and levers. They gave you some privacy, not like these cheap little desks. And they were simple to operate: you saw the guy's name, you pulled the lever next to it. Here you have to get the form, insert it, punch it and then bring it back. Why do they have to complicate things so goddamn much?

"Okay Frances, we put it in like this. Like this. And now we look for Al Gore. There it is. Now take this puncher, take this puncher, like this, like this, hold it like this, and punch the dot. There. THERE! Good. Now, Curtis Imrie. Where is that? Must be on the other ballot. Jesus Christ. This is so goddamn difficult. There. I'll put this in. Take the puncher, take the puncher, and punch again. There. There. Good." We won't do the judges and all this initiative crap, we'll be here all day.

"Take your ballot, Frances, and put it in the box. Here, let me help you. There. Now stand over here while I vote, and then we'll go." "She had a stroke. You want to sit down over here." "She can sit down here? Thank you."

FATHER

MOTHER

It's a couple of school days before Spring vacation. My cousin Florence will arrive on Saturday, and we're going to take the train to San Francisco on Monday. This will probably be our last trip together, as she's getting married in June. I suppose I should be more excited about our trip. We always have such fun together.

I'm meeting Mr. Damasio, Tomas, tonight. He's going to Atlanta to visit his sister, so this will be the last time I see him for over a week. I'm wondering about the summer. I'm going to Missouri for Flo's wedding in June, but I'm not sure if I should then go on home to Illinois, or come back here. It would be nice to see Ma and Pa, and it would be much less expensive to live at home. But Lowell will be on his ship, and there's not much for me to do in Barry Illinois over the summer. Except to get in Ma's hair. If Mr. Damasio plans to keep courting me, I'd like to be where he can. I know girls have been getting married later because of the war, but I'm nearly thirty-one and I'd like to start a family soon. Mabel Dodge already has two boys, and Harriet Sweeney has six, three and three. I guess I'm putting the cart before the horse. I know Tomas likes me. I don't know if he wants to marry me.

We're going to the Howard Johnson's restaurant in Carlin.

168

I hope he takes me to the Bide-A-Wee in Battle Mountain. I'm such a bad girl. I know these feelings are sinful because we're not married, but the way he touches me, I could just melt. But it's a school night, so we'll probably just kiss in his car up on Indian View Hill. Kissing isn't sinful. I wonder if second base is sinful. I can't wait until tonight.

We're driving down the highway to Hunter. I'm wearing my nice brown wool suit, stockings, my white pumps with brown toes and a white cotton blouse with the turquoise earrings that Tomas gave me for Christmas. He even noticed that I don't have pierced ears, like the fast girls. The turquoise looks good against my red hair. Even Miss Sally Jeffers, one of the boarders at Mrs. Henry's, complimented me when I wore them in January. I haven't had my hair done for over a week, and although I worked on it for a while after school it just wouldn't behave. Tomas is wearing a blue suit, a white shirt and a dark blue tie. He hasn't said much. He must be thinking about something else.

"Would you like some music, Frances?" I nod, and he leans over and turns the radio on. At first, it's just country-and-western music, which I don't particularly care for. He adjusts the tuner, and Nat King Cole's voice fills the car. I like Nat King Cole, and quietly hum along. We keep driving.

I'm trying to relax. I lean back in my seat, but can't quite get comfortable. Something seems a little wrong. I look over at Mr. Damasio. He's staring straight ahead, driving. I can't imagine why he'd be angry with me. Maybe it's something with his sister. I know she's been ill. I can't put my finger on it, but something is definitely amiss. I suppose he'll tell me if he wants to. When he's ready. I look out the window and listen to the radio. Nat King Cole changes to the Mills Brothers, "Shine little glowworm, glimmer, glimmer." It gets dark much later than before. It must really be springtime. I wonder why he's taking this exit. It would be faster to continue on the highway. He pulls off to the side of Maggie Creek Ranch Road. He turns the car off. Then the lights. Does he want to make love right here? We sit there in the fading light and wait. He doesn't look at me.

"Damn!" he says, and pounds the steering wheel. I jump a little in my seat. "Damn, damn, damn." "What's wrong?" Is it something I did? "Oh Frances. I need a drink. And you will too. Please take the bottle out of the glove compartment, help yourself if you'd like, and then hand it to me." I do as he asks, but don't take a drink. He looks at me. "Are you sure you don't want a drink? A cigarette?" I shake my head no. What is it? He sighs. "I received a letter yesterday afternoon, a nasty, hurtful, cowardly letter, written in feminine script. It was unsigned." He takes a sip from the whisky bottle. "It read, as nearly as I can remember, for I burned the damn thing in my grate last night, something like 'I know about the filthy fornicating you and Miss Patterson are indulging in. The children of Elko require and deserve better moral direction from their educators. You will be given the opportunity to cease such lascivious behavior. If you and Miss Patterson do not stop rutting around in depravity and corruption, your principal, members of the school board and citizens of your community will be informed.' I take it you have been spared this charming missive?" I feel sad, angry and frightened, all at once. "No, I haven't seen anything like that." I feel tears forming behind my eyes. "Whoever sent this could make trouble for us. Especially for you." "Why especially for me?" "Who was it said that men live by their reputations, while women perish by theirs?" He takes out his handkerchief and dabs at my eyes. "Don't cry Frances.

170

Do you regret anything we've done? Do you feel guilty, wicked or ashamed?" I shake my head and manage to speak. "No. No, no, no. Not at all. No."

He takes a swig from the whisky bottle and stares ahead. Night has almost fallen now. I can hear cars zooming by on the highway. Finally he turns back to look at me. "Good, for I don't feel guilty, ashamed or wicked either. Not in the least." He turns away and starts the car. "Paul Whiteman for the Luxury Nash" blares out, and is quickly switched off. "We'll figure something out when we return from our vacations. Are you hungry? I'm suddenly starving."

"Have you heard the news?" "No, what?" "Mr. Damasio resigned. He's going to care for his sister in Atlanta. She has cancer. Mr. Kelling is trying to get permission to hire a substitute, but if he can't, we're all going to have to take his pupils."

FATHER

Dear Frances, I hope you have a nice birthday. I think of you and remember the good times we had teaching at…what was the name of that school? It wasn't Beulah Heights, Christ, that was her last school, I used to pick her up every day there, Lakeview, that's it, at Lakeview. Love, no, not love. Sincerely, no, no, how about your friend, yes yes, your friend Mrs. Anderson, no not Mrs., too formal. What was her first name? Mrs. Anderson, Mrs. Anderson, I can't remember anything, God damn it, Catherine, that's it, Catherine Anderson. Dear Frances, Happy Birthday. What else? I should have used a different color pen, although she's probably not going to notice. This ain't going to do no good. You'd think her friends would ask how she's doing, contact her, a note, a phone call, something. But no, nothing. Not even on her birthday. Neighbors she's known for twenty, thirty years, never go see her or ask me how she's doing. They're all scared. They don't like to think about it, they don't like to think about it, that's why. At least Jeff always sends a card. And her cousin Harry always sends a letter. Let's see. Dear Frances, Happy Birthday. I hope you enjoy yourself and feel better soon. Best wishes, who? Mrs. Bernard? What's her first name? Lillian? Marilyn? I don't know, I just don't know. Where's the phone book? This is hard on me, hard on me. I'm an old man. It wasn't supposed to be like this. All that money we saved, and those nursing home bastards eat it up. For what? For basic board and room. Bernard...Bernard, why do they make the print of these phone books so small, Bernard, Lillian, I was right. Best wishes, Lillian Bernard. I bought three cards; I should have only bought two. Maybe I could take this one back. $2.50. That's a lot of money for a card. I'll take it back. This is hard on me, hard on me being a caregiver. No one realizes it. And Jeff doesn't help. It's all up to me. Got the candy, the cards, my keys. Make sure to lock up the house, front door, screen door, back door, side door and garage door, don't want any sneak thieves to come in and rob me blind.

I'll park here, out of the way, don't want to get Big Red smashed. What are you looking at? Too many generals here, and not enough soldiers. No one to do the work. Same thing when I was in the army: all these paper pushers and no foot soldiers. And I'm paying almost a thousand dollars a month for it, for basic board and room. Plus the three grand insurance. Almost four thousand for what? It's my fault, I should have gotten that inflation clause. I didn't ask. I assumed, I assumed. I didn't ask.

There's Mrs. Scaplo from the old neighborhood. She's got those swollen ankles, Jesus. "How ya doing, Mrs. Scaplo?" "Yeah, I'm here to see my wife. She had a stroke." I tell her that every time I see her, I guess her memory's not so good. "Okay, see ya later Mrs. Scaplo." "Mr. Fernandez, it's good to see you Mr. Fernandez." "Oh, you're not feeling too good, huh?" "You had an operation last month." "Your kidneys huh?" "You hang in there, Mr. Fernandez, you hang in there." Jesus God this place depresses me. Everybody's got their problems, everybody's got their problems. What about me? I got my problems too. I got a wife who's losing her mind, and who's costing me almost four thousand dollars a month. Four thousand dollars for basic room and board. Mrs. Pino wheels toward me, she's a friend of Jay's. I think her daughter went to South High with Jeff. "Mrs. Pino, Mrs. Pino. Joe DeShell." "Yeah, I'm doing okay, doing okay." "You think I look nice?" "I try to dress up everyday." "I need a haircut huh?" Old nosy bitch. "You sound like my sister. Bye Mrs. Pino." I never liked that woman. She was always bossy, like my sister, always telling everyone what to do. Her husband died last year, now she's got no one to boss. Her daughter lives in California or something. Some of these old people got nobody to visit them, so I try to be friendly. But it's hard on me, hard on me. I never wanted to be a caregiver, I never wanted to be a caregiver. Where's Frances? There's Mrs. Barella. She's only sixty, but lost both legs to the diabetes. She got no legs, no family to take care of her, but she's always cheerful. She keeps on eye on Frances. "How ya doing, Mrs. Barilla?" "You're looking good yourself." "You're right, she's eighty-one today." "She still eating good, huh Mrs. Barella?" "Okay, bye." Some have lost mobility, some an arm or a hand or some other organ inside. And some have lost their minds. Like my wife. This is nothing but a warehouse of rotting people.

There she is, sitting there in her wheelchair, looking out the window. At least they put a nice dress on her. She doesn't recognize me. Forty some years with a person and they don't recognize you. "Frances. Frances. It's your birthday. You got some cards, and Jeff and his wife will be here later. They're coming down from Boulder. You remember me? Do you know who I am?" Nothing. Just that blank stare, looking up at me, then out the window again. I can't tell if it's her or this whole place, but I smell urine. I always have to tell them, "Take her

174

to the bathroom, she's not going to ask, take her to the bathroom." All these generals, and they don't pay the people who change and feed them; they're the ones who should be making the money, not these paper pushers. Just like the army.

I'll ask the charge nurse how she's doing and to get someone to change her. There's Mrs. Montoya, the bitch. Paper pusher. Asked me if I was still working. Of course I'm working, I'm a busy man. That's why I still wear my real estate pin: I want them to think I'm still functioning, still out there in the world. I want them to know this is hard on me, a man with a career. "Hello Mrs. Branby, how's Frances, Mrs. DeShell doing? She's doing about the same, huh? Good appetite, huh? No change or anything? About the same? Yes, it's her birthday. She eats everything on her plate still, huh? Could you get someone over there, Mrs. Barnby, to change her? Ha ha, every time I come here it seems she needs changing. I guess its just coincidence, huh? Thank you Mrs. Barnby. And Mrs. Barnby, I meant to ask you, do you think she'll ever get better?"

No one knows anything. I ask the doctors, they act like they're doing me a favor just to talk to me, and then they don't say nothing. Dementia, dementia, yeah she's got dementia, but what does that mean? I've been reading about the drugs: can't she take some of those new drugs? I read about them in *Time* magazine, the new drugs for Alzheimer's. No one tells me nothing. "Frances. Frances. Happy birthday. Do you recognize me?" I'll wheel her over to the TV room; maybe we'll go to the library. It's private but it has windows and it's right up front, so the generals can see I'm here, taking care of my wife. I should have brought her a coke or a hamburger or something. God she looks bad. Her face is all dry and her teeth are dirty. Four thousand a month for simple board and room: the bastards are going to bleed me dry. I'll have to tell Mrs. Barnby to check on her teeth. "Here Frances, you want a piece of candy? That's it. Good huh? Oh, oh, let me get a napkin. I'll pick it up. No, you don't want that, it's been on the floor. Here, have another piece. I'll throw this one away." I wonder if my sister's been here today: she doesn't come much since Ted died, but maybe because of Frances' birthday. Eighty-one years old. She doesn't deserve this. She should have gone to Hawaii instead of sitting here and looking out the window all day. I don't deserve this either, God I don't deserve this. I should get her some water or something.

"You got some cards today, Frances, for your birthday. Look. Look. Let me read them to you."

MOTHER

It's quiet here now but the students were really wild to-day. Donald Johnson called Vernon Sample a nasty name during reading, and then Rosa Martinez said Lillian McPherson spilled finger-paint on her new dress on purpose, and then Lillian McPherson called Rosa Martinez a dirty lying Mexican. Rosa's twin brother, Hector, heard that and punched Lillian McPherson on the arm. I marched Donald, Rosa, Lillian and Hector to Mr. Simmons' office myself, and when I returned, someone had drawn a picture of me with big breasts on the chalkboard. I didn't say anything. I just erased it and called on Pedro Sanchez to read. The weather has been bad, and they've had to play inside for almost a week straight. And it's only a week and a half to Christmas vacation, so it's probably mostly cabin fever. Still, the kids were never this naughty in Fulton.

I'm going home for Christmas. I like that song, "I'll be home for Christmas, if only in my dreams." My brother Lowell will be there. I haven't seen him in such a long time. When he was in the navy he wrote a postcard to me every single Christmas day, no matter where he was. I have cards from Japan, Korea and some islands that I've never even heard of. I even have some paper money from Japan that Lowell says is worth about six cents. It will be wonderful to see him and his new girlfriend,

Kay. I take the train to Salt Lake City, then to Denver, then to Chicago and down to Saint Louis, where Pa said he'd pick me up. I love taking the train. I love sitting up in the observation car, eating an apple or something, and watching the mountains with the snow all around. I like eating in the dining car too, although that can get expensive. I was hoping my cousin Florence would meet me in Denver, but she's decided to stay in Fort Hayes for the holidays with her fiancé's family. Lucky girl. Flo and I had such a great time taking the train to Washington DC last summer to see the White House, the Capitol, and the Lincoln and Washington Memorials. And then she came out here when I moved to help me get settled. We have such fun together. She's supposed to get married next June. I wonder if I'll be her bridesmaid.

I can't seem to concentrate. I'll have to mark these spelling papers at home. I was always good at spelling. Spelling and attendance. I wonder if Mr. Damasio has gone home yet. We're going to another movie this weekend. It's all very exciting, but I'm not real sure what's happening. I know I have my reputation to protect and all, especially being a schoolteacher, but sometimes when I'm with him, I just melt. I've done that, that thing before, with Terry, a boy from my high school who was going off to the war, and with Harold, a boy at college. I'm thirty-one years old, after all. It wasn't that great. But with Mr. Damasio, Tomas, I sometimes want to try it again. It's what all the songs are about. Maybe we could get married and we wouldn't have to worry about what people would say. Florence could be *my* bridesmaid. I hope I'm not too old.

"Did you like the movie, Miss Patterson, Frances?" We're sitting in Mr. Damasio's 1948 Mercury Coupe, on the Indian View overlooking the town. Patti Page is singing "The

Tennessee Waltz." I'd prefer Christmas music. I'm not all that fond of Patti Page. "I did like the movie. I loved it when Gene Kelly asked the older woman, Milo, what was holding her dress up, and she tells him 'modesty.' That was clever." Maybe I shouldn't have said that. "I also liked when Gene Kelly danced on the piano at the end. 'Tra-la-la-la, this time it's really love, tra-la-la-la.'" Maybe I shouldn't have said that, either. "Did you like the movie?" "I'm not sure yet. I adored that long dance sequence at the end, with all those classical painting references. I'm a big fan of Gershwin, so I quite enjoyed the music. It was definitely cheerful, wasn't it? I guess I'm unconvinced by the story. Gene Kelly is such a rube, and I can't imagine any self-respecting Frenchwomen would have much to do with him. I simply cannot envision a young Lise responding to his harassment in any way other than calling for a gendarme, and to picture a sophisticated and beautiful society *dame* such as Milo granting the time of day to the brutish American hick is beyond my powers of creative ingenuity. He can dance, that's true, but no one in film seems less of a painter to me. The thing was just so damn happy. Although after the war, I guess we have a right to be happy. If we can ignore the Russians, of course. And the Chinese."

I love to hear him talk. I could just listen to him forever. He sounds vaguely like my cousin Jem, from Saint Louis, although Mr. Damasio's accent is smoother, more refined. He moves across the front seat and puts his arm around me. I don't mind at all. He has such gorgeous eyes, so dark and sleepy. I never saw eyes like that in Hannibal Missouri. Patti Page fades out and Dinah Shore, "Sweet Violets," comes in. We can see the twinkling lights of the town from the hill. There's a light coverlet of snow on the ground, gray in the moonlight, and the sky is clear. And cold. I snuggle up closer to Mr. Damasio.

I can smell the tobacco from the cigarettes he smokes. Lucky Strike means fine tobacco. And Ivory soap. "Ah Frances, forgive me for raining on your parade. The film was enjoyable, the company more so." He kisses the top of my head. He is so different from all the other men I've gone with. I wish we could spend Christmas together. Maybe in a mountain cabin, all snowed in. He moves his face toward me and kisses me gently. I want him so. He stops kissing me and smiles. "Ah, where are my manners? Would you like a drink?" I can see his breath. He leans over my knee and takes a flask from the glove compartment. He opens the cap and offers it to me. Yuck, whisky. I take a small drink and hand it back to him. He takes a swig, replaces the cap, and kisses me again. My heart is beating so fast. He opens his mouth. I open my mouth too. I'm melting into his body.

Father

Merry Christmas, Merry Christmas. Jeff should have stayed longer. With his wife and those goddamn dogs. They can't wait to go back to Boulder. Ah hell. This is a nice bottle of whisky. Jim Beam, that's a good brand. I wonder how much he paid for it. He's always splashing his money around. He was always like that. Big spender, big spender. When he moved back from college one summer I found a cancelled check for a hundred and fifty dollars to a liquor store. He said he was having a party. A hundred and fifty dollars.

That Red Lobster, that was nice. Probably cost fifty, sixty bucks for the three of us. I haven't eaten so much in months. I don't get hungry that much anymore. I'm losing weight: my pants don't fit me. Jay's always after me, but what can I do? I don't want to buy new pants. She gave me a couple of pair of Ted's pants, nice pants, but they don't fit me no more. I need a new belt too. I'm just not that hungry. I didn't have much today, just a salami sandwich and some potato chips. And I don't like to go out by myself all the time. You go to a restaurant, you want someone to sit with, to visit with, that's why you go to a restaurant. That was good last night. I had some lobster, a couple of beers, and sat with Jeff and his wife. I'll turn on my Mexican music, and maybe have a drink of my whisky. That will put me right to sleep. Feliz navidad.

I don't need a drink right now. Let me write the date on this bottle, and then put it up in the whisky cupboard. I remember Jeff stole a small bottle of whisky and then sold it to one of the neighbor boys. A five-buck bottle of whisky he sold for a dollar. I remember selling whisky and wine for Mr. Giarantano in the old neighborhood. Where's my pen? Christmas, 2002, Thursday, December 26th, what time did he come, around four thirty, 4:30 pm, from Jeff, #1 Son. I'll pull this chair up, and hold on to the refrigerator. Oh God. Open the cupboard, there…whoa fuck.

Oh Jesus oh Jesus what happened. Oh God oh God. Oh my head. My back. Am I going to die? I can move. I can move. I better call someone. I need to stand up. Jesus what happened? I must have fallen off the chair. What's that? My head, my head's bleeding. I better call the emergency. I'll stay down here for awhile, gather my strength. Jesus God Jesus God. I better get up, I better call someone. Let me lean on the table, let me stand up here. Oh my head hurts. Let me call Jay. Oh God. Five six four oh nine five two. Oh Jesus. Oh God. "Hello Jay. This is Joe. I fell off a chair and I need to go to the emergency. I'm at home I'm at home. Where do you think I am? I fell and I need to go to the emergency. My head's bleeding. You'll call the ambulance. Thank you bye." I'd better sit down.

"Dr. Samuel Smith." "No, no, I haven't been eating much: I haven't been hungry." "I guess I've lost a little weight." "I don't know." "I don't know, maybe two or three months." "You're going to need to take a blood test, huh?" "I fell off a chair. I was putting a bottle of whisky in a cupboard over the refrigerator, and I was hanging on to the door, and it flew open and I fell off the chair. How stupid." "No, no, I wasn't drinking the whisky.

I didn't even open the bottle. My son gave it to me, he's a professor at the University of Colorado. In Boulder, yeah." "No, I don't drink much." "No." "I look a little yellow, huh?" "I've been a little tired lately, yeah. My wife's in a nursing home, and I'm taking care of her." "No, she's at the nursing home, but I go see her, I check up on her. That's a hard job. It's hard on me. She has Alzheimer's." "You're going to take some blood from my arm. Okay." "You want me to make a fist." "No, I don't feel good." "No." "My sister. She's here somewhere." "What's that for? Why are you shining that light in my eyes?" "Concussion, huh. Oh God." "No, I don't feel sleepy. My back's sore and my head hurts." "No, just the top of my head." "No, no dizziness." "I feel sore, and kinda funny, you know?" "*Cat* scan? What's that?" "Concussion, huh? I have a concussion." "You're going to see if I have a concussion, oh." "They'll take me for the scan and then you'll see me later." "Will I be able to go home tonight?" "No, you're going to keep me overnight." "Maybe a couple of days, huh." "Okay doctor, okay. Thank you."

Jesus, a concussion. I hope I don't start losing it like Frances. That's when she started going downhill, when she took that fall at the Colorado Springs airport. I should have sued the bastards. My back hurts; he didn't even look at my back. And my head. I had some bumps up there before. Thank God I have insurance. The bill is probably up to two or three thousand already. The ambulance was three hundred at least. I could have walked out into the van, but they made me lie down on their cart there. Goddamn neighbors got a show. When they took Frances from the nursing home to the hospital after they broke her arm, it was three hundred thirty or three hundred forty, I can't remember. Jesus Christ I can't remember. I remember I mailed them a money order, and then the insurance sent me a check, but I don't remember if it was three thirty or three forty. I don't want to die. I hurt all over. I guess that's a good sign. How stupid. How stupid I was climbing on that chair. I'm thirsty. There's my sister.

"They think I have a concussion, and they're going to run some tests." "Oh, you know huh. You talked to the doctor." "They're going to keep me here a couple of days you think." "You called Jeff but got his answering machine." "I don't know what I was thinking Jay, I don't know." "Yeah, thank you for all you've done, thank you." "I know it's hard after Ted died, and I know your neck is hurting, I know it Jay, I know it." "Thank you." "What time is it?" "Ten thirty already." "Yeah, you go home." "I guess I'll be okay: what am I going to do?" "You'd better tell Jeff to come down." "I'm waiting for them to do a scan, to see if I have a concussion." "No." "Tell that nurse I'm thirsty."

MOTHER

I'm pleased my trunk came today. I was getting tired of wearing the same things: my yellow blouse and skirt, my light blue dress, my nice lilac pattern dress, my orange and crème colored blouse, not to mention having to rely either on my brown-toed pumps or my new white half-heels with those straps that cut into my feet. I'll write Ma a postcard and tell her the trunk arrived safely. It only cost three dollars too.

I'm sure glad I'm going to get paid next week. Two hundred seventy-five isn't much, but it's better than the two hundred thirty I made at Fulton, although Mrs. Henry's boarding-house is fifteen dollars more a month than Mrs. Ferguson's and I don't care for her cooking quite as much. I get paid all twelve months. Maybe I can save some in the summer and travel. I can go to California easily from here on the Greyhound. I'd like to see the ocean, and maybe go to San Francisco and ride a cable car.

It would sure be fine if I could go to San Francisco with Mr. Damasio. He's so handsome and sophisticated, and he makes me laugh. All last week I tried to sit near him in the teacher's room during lunch so I could listen to him tell his funny stories to Mr. Lane. Mr. Damasio was in London England for the war, and he told Mr. Lane a story about how he

185

was on leave one day, and needed some aspirin for a headache, and went to a big department store and one of the clerks told him that the chemist was near the lift, and Mr. Damasio didn't know what he was talking about. The way he said "the chemist was near the lift" was so funny. Mr. Damasio is a sharp dresser. He wears such colorful ties, sometimes even bright red, and he smells good too. I've never met anyone like him. Not in Fulton, and certainly not in Barry, and not even in Quincy. And he's unmarried. I'm not sure I would enjoy going to London if they have all those different words. Mr. Damasio says it's very cold and damp there too. I'd rather go someplace warm and colorful, like Hawaii. I should stop all this daydreaming and work on my lesson plans for school. If I finish up before nine I'll go downstairs to smoke a cigarette and listen to the radio. Maybe the other girls like Charlie Wild too. I keep hearing that Tony Bennett song about melting a cold cold heart. I'll write that postcard to Ma tomorrow, after church. I wish my cousin Florence was still here. The other girls aren't that friendly to me. Maybe they're too busy.

Elko sure is dusty and dry. The temperature is about the same as back home, but it doesn't seem quite as hot here, I suppose because it's drier. I need to go to the drugstore to get some hand lotion. "The chemist near the lift" ha ha. I should look over my lessons before I walk to school, but I need to stop at the post office to mail Ma's card and Lowell's letter before, so I'd best be going now. I am happy to wear low heels today. I was afraid I'd ruin my nice white shoes that weren't even broken in, walking around all this construction. No wonder it's so dusty. I wonder when they're going to finish this sidewalk. They need to plant more trees. I miss all the oaks, maples and willows back home.

Arithmetic is first, then reading, then penmanship. Then lunch. Oh drat, I left my sandwich in the icebox. I guess I'll have to go to Nelson's Drugstore for a hamburger. That's fifteen cents I wasn't planning to spend. And I won't be able to listen to Mr. Damasio tell his funny stories in the faculty room. Oh well. At least I'll be able to pick up some Jergens. I don't like eating lunch alone. Maybe Mr. Damasio will come with me. Ha ha.

"A penny for your thoughts." "Hello Mr. Damasio. I was thinking about, I was thinking about…fractions. I'm teaching fractions today." "Ah, yes, fractions. Making things smaller and smaller. Parts and parts of parts. I hear they're working on this gizmo, no bigger than your fingernail, that will replace all our vacuum tubes." I like the way he's looking at me. He's wearing this beautiful mauve tie. I guess it's my turn to speak. "I've never seen you walk this way to school before, Mr. Damasio." "I don't usually, but I need to go to the p.o. before the first bell. I am mailing a letter to my sister in Atlanta. And you, Miss Patterson? Is this your traditional approach to the schoolhouse?" "Yes, yes it is. I live at Mrs. Henry's boardinghouse on Pine Street, near 13th. I walk this way every day." "So what do you think of our fair town, Miss Patterson? You hail from Illinois, if I'm not mistaken. What are your impressions of our small burg, Elko Nevada?" "It's very nice. The people are very friendly. I've always lived in small towns, and I guess I prefer the quiet. Are you from around here?" "I did attend the teacher's college here, but originally I'm from Atlanta. Atlanta Georgia. And yes, Elko is a small, quiet town…sometimes a bit too quiet."

We stop in front of the post office. Mr. Damasio pats his coat jacket and frowns. He holds the door open for me, and as I step by him he says, "Miss Patterson, a moment please. May

I call on you, perhaps this weekend? Perhaps for a movie?" I look at him. He's very handsome, with his crinkly blue eyes and small moustache. Things are more liberal here than in Fulton, but I don't think we're supposed to "date" our fellow teachers. But a movie, what would be the harm? It would be very nice to talk to someone besides the other teachers or Mrs. Henry. And he is so funny. And if he thinks its okay, then it must be. "Yes, Mr. Damasio, you may call on me this weekend." He smiles. "I seem to have forgotten my letter. I'll wait out here for you." I hurry into the post office.

FATHER

Where am I? Where am I? I'm still in Saint Mary Corwin. Oh Mary mother of God. I don't feel well. My head's killing me, and my back, oh my back. How stupid that was. How stupid. Let me sit up. Oh God. I got this needle in my arm. What's that for? I wonder if they gave me something to knock me out. I wonder if I'm going to die. I'm not ready, I'm not ready. Sweet Jesus.

"Hey Dad, how you doing?" It's Jeff, my son. "Hello." He takes my hand. He looks just like my brother. Babe was so smart. I'm so proud of my son. "Hello Mr. DeShell." His wife, Lisa. She's a smart one, too smart to have children. I should have gone to their wedding. Why didn't I go? I couldn't leave my house. I couldn't get off the block. Oh God. I'm a failure, and now I'm going to die. "We heard you took a little tumble." I nod. I'm thirsty, is there any water around? "What were you doing, trying to put the whisky above the fridge? You need to watch yourself." My mouth's so dry I can't speak. Jeff leans down. "Have you spoken to a doctor yet? Do you know what's going on?" I don't know anything. They thought I had a concussion. "No. Do I have a concussion?" I'm so thirsty. I turn to the right, away from Jeff, but there's no water on the little table next to me. "No, you don't have a concussion. You

189

have jaundice, Dad. One or both of your bile ducts is blocked. That's why you're so yellow." Jaundice. Oh God. One of my army buddies, I can't remember the name, had the jaundice from malaria. Jaundice: that's bad. "I need some water." Jeff looks around. His wife gets up and says, "I'll go get the nurse." "Jaundice. Is that bad?" Jeff looks down. "It could be gall-stones. It could be something more serious." Cancer. Oh God I have cancer. Like my sister Ange. They found the cancer in her pancreas and nine months later she was dead. I don't want to die. I don't want to have the cancer.

I've wasted my life. I wanted to make something out of it, to be a lawyer and fight for civil rights, but the army came and took me. I was young, so young, all I wanted was to chase girls, but the army took me and shipped me off. I could never get back on track after that. They really fucked me up. And I married two women who were no good for me. It wasn't their fault: I should have been alone. The only good thing I ever did was make a son. A Fulbright winner and a professor. And I was never a good father to him. Never. And now I've got cancer and I'm going to die. He's the only good thing I ever did. I need to tell him, I need to tell him. He looks so much like Babe. Babe was the smart one. He went through Fort Benning Officer's School in peacetime, that's how smart he was. That goddamn gambling. Jeff looks just like him. "You look just like my brother, Jeff, just like my brother Babe. God he was smart. He went through Fort Benning. But the gambling, the gambling got him. You know how important he was to me, and you're just as important Jeff, just as important." I'm such a failure, such a failure.

"Hello there, Mr. DeShell. Your daughter-in-law says you need some water. Let me check your chart and see what the doctor says. I don't see anything here about restricting your fluids—sometimes with liver problems they restrict your water intake—no, I don't see anything on your chart. Oh wait, I see. They're going to have you scoped this morning. Mr. DeShell, they're going to stick a tube down your throat and look around to see what they can see. You can't have any water until after that." "Can I have some water?" "No Dad, she just said you can't have any water." "No Mr. DeShell, I'm afraid I can't give you any water. They'll be coming soon to scope you. They should be here in fifteen minutes or so."

"Do you understand what's happening? Your ducts are blocked, and they can't see why, so they're going to stick a tube down your throat and look around." "I don't want to die, Jeff, I don't want to die." "Let's see what's going to happen. They don't know what's causing the blockage. When did you have your gallbladder removed?" "I still got my gallbladder." "Are you sure? The doctor said he couldn't see it." "I got my gallbladder. I never had nothing taken out." I want a drink of water. "Is it going to hurt, this tube?" "I imagine they'll put you to sleep." "They could find cancer, couldn't they?" "Let's just wait until they check it out. It could be nothing, it could be just stones." But they could find the cancer. Oh God. I was never a good man, not a good husband, and not a good father. Now I'm going to die of cancer. "I wasn't a very good father to you, was I Jeff?" Why won't he look at me? "Answer me, I wasn't a good father, was I?" He shrugs. "You were all right." I was a lousy father, and a lousy husband too. I'm going to die a lousy man. I'm going to die a lousy man.

"It's okay Dad, it's okay." "You know how much I respected my brother, and you're just like him, just like him. You're like your mother too, a teacher, a noble profession. Just like your mother. We were so proud of you, your mother and I. You and your wife, Lisa, where is she…?" "I'm right here."

191

"You and your wife, both Fulbright winners. And I should have come to your wedding, I should have come. That's my biggest regret, not coming to your wedding. But I couldn't get off the block Jeff, I couldn't get off the block." "It's okay Dad, it's okay." "And now I have the cancer." Oh God, Oh God. Oh sweet Jesus God. Now I have the cancer and I'm going to die. Why does everything happen to me? First Frances getting Alzheimer's and now I get cancer. Everything happens to me. God why do you hate me? Life is not fair. Life is not fair. "Calm down Dad, calm down. The doctors don't know anything yet." He hands me a tissue. My eyes are wet. I dry my eyes and face. I need to pull myself together.

"Okay Mr. DeShell, time to go." Two young Mexican men are standing in the doorway with a cart. Jeff gets up. "We're going to transfer you to this gurney and take you down to have them prep you for surgery." Jeff squeezes my hand as they lift me out of the bed.

MOTHER

"Look Frances, look at all the cars and trucks. Looks like the entire county's here. There's Albert and Ruby's old Ford Model A, and Uncle Chauncy's flatbed. There's Josiah's new yellow Nash." "That's a Standard Six. Not a bad car." "I wonder where he got the money for it." "Probably from his daddy." "Some folks got it." "And some don't." "I see the sheriff's car." "Yeah, I reckon he'd be here. Probably brought a few deputies too." "You think there'll be trouble?" "Naw, there ain't going to be trouble. This many people, he just wants to play it safe." "There's Tom Rawlins' truck." "I thought Martha was sick." "She may very well be but that looks like Tom's truck. Don't that look like Tom's DeMartini, Ray?" "It does." "Maybe she's feeling a whole lot better." "Last I heard, she was in the hospital in Springfield. And I didn't hear that she came out yet." "You know Tom, always willing to help out." "He should help out his own kin first." "Now Maggie, we don't know the man's business." "I'm just saying, take care of your own kin first." "What's that supposed to mean? You don't think we should be here? Helping out?" "I'm just saying, if Roy Newsome hadn't wanted to be all high and mighty he wouldn't have got himself, and his family, into this bank mess. Nobody forced him to buy half of Jason's farm. And without the cash money to do so. So

193

he borrows from the bank. And what does he need to farm all that new land? A couple of new John Deeres and a cultivator. Again, no cash money. So he visits Mr. Oliver Warbucks at the bank again. Three bad years and here we are. The entire county out to save his hide. I don't see Ray and Helen traipsing down to the Security Bank every time they want a new winter coat or new Zenith radio. You take care of your own kin first. I ain't going to say another word about it." Ma sounds mad. I'm excited. I've never been to an auction before. "Lowell still sleeping, Maggie?" "Yes he is." "I'm just going to pull in here."

It's cold and rainy outside, but the barn is warm and dry. It smells like dry hay, corn, horses and people. I wonder where the horses are now. There's a crowd of folks here, and I have to stand on my toes to see. Ma, Lowell and Aunt Helen are in the back, sitting on a bale of hay, but I'm with Pa and Uncle Ray near the front because I don't want to miss whatever's going to happen. I see my uncle Chauncy and cousin Harry, Mr. and Mrs. Hales, Susan Kay and Betty Ann McCleery with their dad, and a group of strangers in dark city clothes in the corner near the birthing stall. Mr. Newsome is talking to Mr. Rawlins near a long table set out near the big double doors. I don't see Mrs. Rawlins or Mrs. Newsome or Janey and Pete. I never liked Janey. She's mean. She once called Ellen Perry a P-I-G pig right to her face and said she was sure glad she had nice store-bought dresses to wear to school, and not some farmhand stockings and seed-bag shifts like some girls wore. Lewis Boyd and Evan Goodfellow started laughing, and Ellen Perry ran off crying. Miss Forbes came over and asked what was wrong with Ellen Perry, and I didn't want to tattle, so I didn't say anything. There's the sheriff. He's standing with this small man in a city hat who looks like he'd rather be somewhere else.

Mr. Prentiss, the auction caller, walks up to the table, takes out this little hammer from a small drawstring bag, and hits the table a couple of times. He's wearing his dark Sunday suit. Everyone gets quiet. "I reckon you all have had a chance to look over whatever it is you were going to look over, so we'll get started. We'll commence by taking bids on the farm tools and implements, then the vehicles, then the household furnishings, fixtures, utensils, appliances and accessories, then the livestock, tack and feed, then the structures, including the farmhouse and all the outbuildings, and finally the land by lots. So we're going be here a while." Mr. Prentiss stops and looks around. "Okay. First item up for bid is that four-year-old IHC two-row tractor-mounted corn-picker, with accessories and mounting hardware, lot number one. OkaywhatamIbidamIbid fiveamIbidfiveamIbidfivefivefiveyesfivetoyouthat'sfivecent toyousiramIbidsixsixsixamIbidsixsixsixanyonesixsixsixonce twicefivethreetimessoldtothatgentlemanovertherefforfive cents." BANG. That was so fast. A couple of the strangers look at each other and then begin to yell. The sheriff steps forward and says, "Quiet, quiet please: we're trying to run this peaceful like." They swallow their yelling and grumble low. I wonder why those men are so angry. "Let's move on to item number two. This is a ten-year-old seven-foot tandem disk from John Deere. It's just the tandem disc and nothing else. SowhatamIbidforthissevenfoottandemdiskwhatamIbiddoI hearfour?" The men by the birthing shed start yelling but Mr. Prentiss talks louder, "doIhearfourfourfour?" "Four!" my pa yells, "IgotfourdoIhearfivedoIhearfivedoIhearfive?" "Five dollars, five DOLLARS!" one of the strange men yells but Mr. Prentiss isn't paying him any mind. "DoIhearfivedoIhearfive doIhearfive?" "Five DOLLARS, FIVE DOLLARS, do you hear me!" "DoIhearfivedoIhearfivefivefivefiveonceatfourtwice

195

atfour…" "FIVE DOLLARS YOU CHEAT…" "Soldtothat gentlemanforfourcents" BANG.

The men by the birthing shed are grumbling louder now, and that man in the city hat is hopping around, looking as mad as a chicken with its head cut off. I tug on Pa's hand. He leans down to me. "Pa, why did you buy that tandem disc? We don't have a farm." Pa looks down at me. "I'll tell you later, Frances. Keep your ears and eyes open for now." Why didn't Mr. Prentiss sell it to that man who bid five whole dollars for it? "This here's lot number two, a collection of twelve rakes, daisy rakes, hay rakes and hay forks, all less than five years old, most from Sears Roebuck. Lot number two, twelve rakes and forks." "CanIgettwocanIgettwocanIgettwocomeonfolksgivemetwo givemetwogivemetwo." "Two." "IgottwotwotwotwotwocanIget threethreethreeanybodygivemethree?" "One dollar." "CanIget threethreethree?" "ONE DOLLAR!" CanIgetthreethreethree threethree?" BANG. "Sold for two cents." I forget and ask Pa, "Who are those strangers over there by the birthing shed? The ones who look all mad?" "Those fellows over there want to buy up his farm and take it, but Mr. Prentiss, he's a good man, Mr. Prentiss, he can't see 'em for some reason. He needs some glasses or something, because he just can't see 'em at all." "And who's that over there? The one hopping around?" "That would be Mr. Samuel Shaw. The banker. He's just trying to do his job." "But he don't have to enjoy it so," says Uncle Ray. "He enjoy it too much." "It don't look like he enjoying it too much now, does he?"

"No, it sure don't," laughs Uncle Ray. "It sure don't."

FATHER

I should eat. I'm not that hungry, but I should eat. I could go down to Tommy the Rock's, but I don't really care for Mexican food. My stomach can't take it any more. Besides, he don't cook much these days, and I don't know where he gets those vecchias he has back in that kitchen. I could go to Jo Jo's, but he charges so much for his damn spaghetti: I don't want to pay fifteen dollars for a plate of homemades and a beer. I can afford it, sure, but I don't want to pay that much. There's Furr's Cafeteria down the street. I don't like having to stand in line with a tray. Reminds me of the army. I'm sick of Burger King. The Whopper. That's insulting. I could go to Whisky Ridge, get me a plate of their spaghetti. But I can't eat it all, and will have to bring some home. When Jeff came down, I ate it up just like that. It's not the food, it's the company. When you have to eat alone, you're just not hungry, you're just not hungry. My sister brings me food sometimes, but she's in Florida. I hope she don't move there permanently. I tell her: "All your friends are here. You have roots in Pueblo. What are you going to do in Florida?" It's been hard on her since Ted died. I know that.

I could go to Kings and get some sausage. And maybe some bread, make myself a sandwich. Then I'd have to fight the crowd at Kings. All those people, all those people. Where do they come from? I should go see Frances too. I haven't been there in a couple of days. I could probably eat at the nursing home for free, but who wants to touch that crap? I'm paying a thousand a month out of our savings, for what? For basic room and board, basic room and board. They don't even give her therapy. It's just a warehouse for old people. That's what I call it, warehousing, warehousing. And that insurance. I'll never get over that. When they said lifetime, I thought it meant for life. Not three years. I blame myself, I should have read the policy. But lifetime is for life! Not three years. In six months, it's going to run out, and then I'm going to have to pay four thousand dollars a month out of my own pocket. For what? For basic room and board. I should have read the policy. I blame myself. But I thought life meant life. And not once has the insurance guy, the guy who sold me the policy, written or called. They get your money, and it's see you later. That nursing home, it's going to bleed me dry. And Frances could live another ten years. Oh God.

And these neighbors, these neighbors, not one has written or called, asking how she is. Not one. After all she did for everyone. All the free babysitting she did for next door. I brought her home once, when Jeff and his wife came down, and I had him walk her down the block. That was when she still could communicate, when she still could walk. I had him walk her down the block and back, with his wife and two dogs, so everyone could see her, so all the neighbors could see her. And they never ask. They never write or call. What are you afraid of?

I had some cornflakes with my coffee this morning, but that was at five, and it's almost twelve now. I'm just not hungry. I could go to McDonald's and then bring Frances a hamburger and a coke. She's already had her lunch, but food is her only treat. Her eyes light up when she sees a hamburger, a cookie or some chocolate. And Jeff. She doesn't recognize me. We lived together over forty years, and she doesn't even know who I am. I sing songs to her, songs of the forties. That's my therapy, singing her the old songs, like "I'll be seeing you in all the old familiar places," or "To spend one night with you, In our old rendezvous, And reminisce with you, That's my desire." I don't know if she remembers them or not. That's my therapy, singing her the old songs. I push her around in her chair, and sing these songs, and everyone gives me the eye, you know. What are you looking at? I don't think it helps her. Maybe it does.

La Famiglia is having a dinner next Saturday at the depot. It was nice last time: linen napkins, good bread, filled water glasses on the table so you don't have to ask, real classy. The food was good too. You got a plate full of spaghetti, gravy, a roll and butter, a salad and a brownie for $6.99 for seniors. I had two beers and got out of there for ten bucks.

There's the mail. Twenty years, they'd come between ten and ten thirty, no matter who was doing the route, and now it's three thirty or four before they come. I called, I called the post office and asked them why it was so late, and they told me there was a route change. Route change. I told them some old people like their mail to come at the same time, it gives their lives routine, it's something to look forward to. "We had to change the route, but if you'd like to inquire, you can call this number in Denver." "What do you think I'm doing," I said, "I'm calling *you* to inquire." I don't know why I bother; all I get is bills and charity solicitations. The askers. Let's see what the askers want today. Disabled American Veterans, American Legion, Frances' retired teachers magazine, Democratic Party of Southern Colorado, what did the Democratic party ever do for me? A credit card application, one for me and one for Jeff,

I wonder how his money's doing, I wonder if he's still got that big debt, United Way, the askers, the askers, Prudential Insurance, what do they want? They want to make sure they got the right address. Of course, you got the right address, I got this didn't I? Look at all this crap. I can't remember the last time I got a personal letter. I can't remember the last time I wrote a personal letter either. I don't even send Christmas cards. I need to get rid of this. Tear it all up. I don't want the government spying on me. I don't want my name at the dump. Tear it up, tear it all up.

I wrote plenty of letters to the newspaper, and to Washington telling them about Babe's case. And that racist *Star Journal* with that Harvard editor wouldn't print any of them. "I can't read your writing" he says. Can't read my writing. Even when I had Frances print it carefully, he still didn't publish it. He just didn't like what I had to say. Cuomo answered me, a form letter with a little note at the bottom, but he answered me. I wrote to the Colorado Attorney General, MacFarlane, and he didn't answer me, that big phony. I even wrote to two US Attorney Generals: Saxbe didn't answer me, and neither did Levi. Bunch of bastards. I want to take Babe's case before the United Nations. I want to expose this racist town of Pueblo Colorado. You talk about human rights in China and Africa, how about looking inside, how about trying to see how Italian-Americans are treated in Colorado. This was my last hurrah, to tell my story, to tell my brother's story, and Frances had to get sick. Why did she have to get sick? That really fucked me up. I was going to make my last hurrah, take my civil rights case to the United Nations, and she had to get sick and really fuck me up. She should have taken that money and lived it up, gone to Hawaii instead of giving it to the nursing home while she rots in there. She should have taken it to Vegas and had some fun instead of being bled by those leeches at the nursing home. I should eat. Maybe I'll go get a Whopper. Or a chicken sandwich.

MOTHER

"C'mon Lowell, we're going to see the kittens. Hurry up. You're slower than molasses in January." "You just say that cause Ma says it." "Hurry up." "Do you think Ma will let us get one?" "Not if they're all gone by the time we get there." "I want a white one, or a gray one with a white tail." "We're not going to get anything unless you hurry. Where are your shoes?"

I like Uncle Ray and Aunt Helen's farm. Their whole farm smells like all different kinds of corn. The outside smells like the sweet corn in the fields, the barn smells like hay mixed with seed corn, and the chicken house smells like cracked corn and chickens. Aunt Helen told Ma that Fibber crawled up in the hayloft to have her kittens, and we have to dress up, so I don't know if we'll be allowed to climb up to see Fibber and her kitties or if Uncle Ray will bring a couple down for us. I don't know why we have to dress up to go to the farm. I hope we can climb up to see Fibber. I hope we can keep one of the kittens.

It's hot in this old truck, with the four of us, Ma, Pa, Lowell and me, squeezed together in the front. It's too hot for this dress. It's the middle of September and it must be ninety degrees. Ma made me wear my blue dress with the big polka dots, the matching jacket *and* the long-sleeve blouse, and my stockings and Mary Janes. "But why do I have to wear a good dress to go to the farm?" "Don't you want to look pretty for Aunt Helen and Uncle Ray?" Lowell's hot too. Even though he has shorts Ma made him button up his collar, put on his jacket and wear his good wool socks. Ma washed and brushed my hair. I like when she does that. She doesn't say much, she just hums, but her humming is like talking. Her humming tells me that she thinks I'm a beautiful lady, or I will be someday.

I like riding out to the farm. I don't like the dusty, bumpy road, but I like looking at the fields of corn and hay, corn and hay. I can see the tall silos of Sweeney's Feed on the left, and here comes the Hoyts' big red house on the right. Sometimes their dog King chases the truck, but he must be taking a nap or something now. I like the way the wind feels on my face. Ma's going to have to brush my hair again.

We turn right past the big willow trees and see Uncle Ray, sitting on the old tractor near the fence. He gives us a little salute and Pa slows down and shouts out, "Anything wrong?" and Uncle Ray shakes his head and then Pa says, "We'll meet you at the house," and Uncle Ray nods and then Pa says to Ma, "That brother-in-law of yours don't say much," and Ma just smiles.

We drive next to the east field and I smell the fresh corn everywhere. I helped detassel this field in July. It was hot then too. I'll never forget that feeling when I grabbed that tassel that was full of corn aphids. It was so disgusting. I don't like detasseling much. Maybe next year I can rogue, like Ethyl and Horace. But I'm tall, one of the tallest girls, so I'll probably detassel again. We came out on Johnson's big wagon, and we had lemonade and cookies like it was a hayride. They tried to make it fun, but it was hard work, and hot. I gave my money to Ma, and she bought me a new straw hat and school pencils with some of it.

The corn is much taller than me now and both Pa and Uncle Ray soon will be working sunup to sundown. I hope nobody dies that week so Pa won't have to take time away from harvesting to dig a grave. Of course, I hope nobody dies anyway, but especially during harvesting week.

We pass the oak trees and the water trough, and the cornfield changes to freshly cut grass. Molly runs up to greet our truck, and I can see Aunt Helen looking out the front window. We wait until Pa stops the truck and then Lowell yells, "Where are the kittens? I want a kitten," and Ma slaps him smartly on the hand. Aunt Helen shuffles out the front door and gives Ma a big hug. "You all want something cold to drink? That truck looks might dusty." "I know where the well is." "Nonsense, Pat, I have some lemonade fresh made." "I want to see the kittens! Where are the kittens?" "Lowell, hush! If'n you don't hush, we'll turn right back around." "We'll see the kittens soon, love, as soon as Uncle Ray gets here to climb up in the loft. Let me look at you, Frances, you look so nice." Ma brushes the hair out of my face with her fingers. We all turn as we hear the old tractor rattle up the driveway and stop near the barn. "Well here's Ray now. Climb on up and bring a couple of them kittens down, will ya!" Ray nods as he gets off his tractor and moves slowly to the barn. "Can we have a kitten Ma? Can we?" " We ain't been offered one, Lowell. Mind your manners." I see Aunt Helen gives Ma a secret look. We're going to get a kitten!

Lowell runs to the fence near the barn. I look up at Ma, who nods, and I skip after him quickly. I hear Aunt Helen say, "I guess the lemonade will have to wait." Lowell is already standing on the second rail. "You kids are in your good clothes now, so stay on this side of the fence." We can see Uncle Ray's boots through the door as he backs down the hayloft ladder. He turns around and we get our first peek at them. They are so small. I can't help myself, step up on the bottom rail, and lean over the fence. He's carrying two in each hand, four tiny balls of fur and closed eyes. They are so small and so cute. He hands one to Lowell and one to me and mine right away starts blindly cuddling in my arms. He sets the other two on the ground in front of Ma, Pa and Aunt Helen. "Watch where you step now," he says. Mine is striped gray and black with a solid black tail. Lowell's is mostly gray and white. I can't believe how soft her fur is. I want this one so bad. I turn to Ma and Pa. "Can we keep one? Please? We'll take care of it. Please?" "Another mouth to feed," says Pa, but then he looks at Ma and gives her that smile with his eyes. "I guess one tiny kitten won't make no difference," Ma says. "If'n you take care of it." "I will I will I promise. Thanks Ma, thanks Pa. Thank you Uncle Ray, thank you Aunt Helen. What you going to do with the rest of these, Uncle Ray?" It's suddenly quiet. Uncle Ray looks down at the ground. "We'll give 'em away to other folks, Frances. Don't you worry about it none."

FATHER

God I'm tired. I need some sleep. I'll turn the air conditioner down and brush my teeth. Three thousand dollars on that air conditioner. Works good. I spent close to fifteen thousand on the house, fixing it up. New carpet, new furniture, new windows, new furnace. Why not? Better than the nursing home getting it, those sons of bitches. Four thousand a month for room and board, four thousand a month. Maybe when Jeff comes down I'll see about that Buick. My Oldsmobile's twenty years old. Big Red. Big Red. Drives good. New car will be an investment.

No more toothpaste. God damn it. When did I buy this tube? June 7th, 2004 at three thirty from King Soopers. Three dollars and twenty-nine cents. God, that's expensive. I remember when toothpaste was a nickel. I'd better put it on the grocery list. Toilet paper, toothpaste, lettuce, salad dressing, chicken, canned soup, a couple of frozen pizzas, ice cream, Aqua Velva shave lotion, three tomatoes, coffee, Jesus I'm out of everything. Good thing tomorrow's Saturday. I'll go early, after I go to the nursing home, push the cart around, take my time. Probably spend seventy, eighty dollars. Better put that on my other list, make out check, grocery shopping. Where's that list? I just saw it, God damn it. There. No, that's next week's list. Cemetery, I haven't been to the cemetery all month. Doctor Smith on Thursday. I go to Doctor Smith, and he talks to me for five minutes. I have to have all my questions written down, and before I get to the second one he's already out in the hall, writing his report. I tell him, I tell him, "Doctor, I get fifteen minutes doctor, I get fifteen minutes." But he's already out in the hall. We don't communicate. Where's my Saturday list? There. Church. If I'm not too tired, I'll go to church tomorrow night. Holy Family has changed. People don't dress up anymore, they look like slobs. I wear a coat and tie, I look nice. I told that priest, I told him, look at these women in slacks, and the men in tee shirts and basketball shorts. Can't we have a dress code? He looked at me like I was out on my balcony. I gave him a dirty look back. The evil eye. I don't care. I like what I am. Women should wear dresses and men should wear hats.

These pajamas feel good. Turn the light out, save on electricity. Draw the curtains, lock the door, okay. I'll turn on my Mexican music and lie down in my chair. I don't feel like listening to those talk shows tonight. They're all alike. Everyone's a bastard. What a stupid war. I'll sit in my leather chair and put my leg up. It's still swollen. I haven't been able to sleep in a bed for years. I hope I can sleep tonight. This is a nice chair. Spent more than two thousand on this new furniture. Italian leather. In the day, it looks brown, and at night, black. I spent two thousand dollars and American Furniture Warehouse don't send me a thank you note, the bastards. Not a phone call or nothing, nothing to say "Hey, Mr. DeShell, we appreciate your business." What time is it? Twelve thirty. Oh God I'm tired.

I should have gone to the nursing home today, see if they fixed Frances' hair. Fifteen dollars a week, and it don't look no better. That place depresses me. The warehouse. The human warehouse. I see people from the old neighborhood,

Box Elder, Abriendo, Elm. I see people from the old neighborhood one week, and they ain't there the next week. My friend, Michael Giaratano, used to live next to Eddie Mastro's parents, he was looking good one day a couple of months ago. I was wheeling Frances up and down the halls, singing her the songs of the forties and fifties, and there's Michael lined up for lunch in his chair, looking like he could still play football. He was in the service with Jo Jo, they went to Guadalcanal together. Jo Jo's closed. After fifty years, he just closed. Never smoked or drank or nothing. I should give him a call. I told him Jay moved to Florida. Next day, I don't see Giaratano, and then I read his obituary on Friday. Heart attack. I should have gone to his funeral.

I don't know why I go to church. What has God done for me? I don't give 'em no money. I don't give nobody nothing no more. Askers. What has the Catholic Church done for me? What has God done for me? Look at Frances. Four thousand dollars a month. Her cousin had Alzheimer's. God I wish she'd get better. That disease really fucked me up. This was supposed to be my golden years, my golden years where I could work on my civil rights. But I have to be a caregiver, a caregiver to a person who's not all there. This is hard on me, this is hard on me. I never wanted to do this. I never wanted to be a caregiver. You'd think Jeff would take more interest, would take more interest in how his mother's being treated. But it's me, it's me who looks her all over, who checks her face for bruises, who goes to the drug store to get her medication so the nursing home won't get their twenty percent markup, those thieving bastards. It's not Jeff, it's me who does all this, me. I ask the hard questions: did you take her to the bathroom? did you brush her teeth? did you put a sweater on her? will you adjust her prosthesis? would you clean that junk out of her eyes?' I ask the questions, the hard questions. They can see me coming. They don't like me and I don't like them. It's an adversarial relationship, that's what it is, an adversarial relationship. I'm paying too much money, over four thousand dollars for basic board and room, and they don't do nothing. I see all the pictures on the wall, all the generals, all the paper pushers, but the soldiers, the ones who change her and feed her, they don't make money, and so they quit. Four thousand dollars a month for a bunch of paper pushers. And I tell them. I do it in a nice way, but I told Mrs. Raiz, I told her, "Why do you have all these administrators, where are the nurses Mrs. Raiz, where are the nurses?" I told her, four thousand dollars is a lot of money, a lot of money. It don't do no good. But they know I'm there, they know I'm there. Who else is going to do it? They don't like me, but I don't give a fuck.

I need my music, I need my music to sleep. Jeff don't come down that much. He calls once a week, for five minutes. You'd think he'd be more concerned about his mother, more concerned about me. We never got along, he and I, we never got along. And that snotty bitch of a wife. He should have married an Italian girl, a girl who did what he wanted her to, a girl who wanted children. I wanted to be a grandfather, I wanted to be a grandfather. I didn't get nothing out of him, I didn't get nothing out of this marriage, this marriage, I didn't get nothing out of this life. I don't get along with nobody. I'm not dying. I like what I am.

I like what I am.